16 Ways to Break a Heart

16 Ways to Break a Heart

LAUREN STRASNICK

KATHERINE TEGEN BOOKS
An Imprint of HarperCollins Publishers

Katherine Tegen Books is an imprint of HarperCollins Publishers.

16 Ways to Break a Heart

www.epicreads.com

[horizontal rule]
ISBN 978-0-06-241872-2
[horizontal rule]

Typography by
17 18 19 20 21 XXXXXX 10 9 8 7 6 5 4 3 2 1
❖

First Edition

[DEDICATION TK]

"You treat me badly; I love you madly."
—Smokey Robinson, "You Really Got a Hold on Me"

"Love is a burning thing."
—June Carter Cash & Merle Kilgore, "Ring of Fire"

1

Dear Dan,

Greetings from the graveyard of ex-girlfriends!

I'm at the coffee shop at Dayview, writing you from that tiny table at the back of the café, the one you hate, the wicker one that wobbles? The place is completely dead. I could've easily sat outside under a pink bougainvillea vine or snagged a window seat looking out onto the quad—instead I'm spilling warm puddles of café au lait all over my best stationery because this shitty little table reminds me of the first time we met. You slammed into me, remember? Knocking me into the creamer and condiment setup. The ultimate meet-cute! Something jazzy and bright pumped out of a stereo speaker, the kind of music that always makes me feel as if I'm sexy and French: a plump-lipped ingenue buying peonies at an open-air market, gnawing on a baguette while smoking Gauloises and reading Proust. You wore your best beret. Okay, not really. You spoiled the fantasy with all your plaid and denim. I liked you anyways. You seemed like the type who'd get misty-eyed watching inspirational sports movies. The kind of guy who loves his mother. Who takes pride in his bear hugs and back rubs, natch.

"Crap!" You'd whacked me upwards and sideways—cream and sugar splattering all over my school uniform. "I'm so sorry," you said as I gracelessly flicked globs of milk from my kilt. "Let me make it up to you? Buy you something nice?"

"A pony?"

You laughed and bought me a coffee instead. I never let anyone buy me anything but our eyes locked and the angels sang and I instantly knew I could love you. Alexa claims she felt something similar once with a guy she met at the food court at the Glendale Galleria. She's wrong. What passed between us that day was a revelation—a revolution? With one lingering look I felt our minds merge and our bodies mash and I swear to God, Dan, I saw prom dresses and promise rings; I watched our twin futures unfurl like a giant architectural blueprint.

We were an inevitability, you and me.

Remember what happened next?

We moved to the tiny table and talked about Dayview. You were an after-school employee; a twice-a-week kind of guy who worked with the kids with the more severe developmental issues.

"What exactly do you do with them?" I asked.

"Mostly just help with the physical stuff: swim club, relay, basketball. Some of the students are pretty strong and hard to manage. I guess I'm

like a teacher's aide."

"I do something similar," I said, even though it wasn't very similar at all. I'd been volunteering in a parent-funded art therapy program at Eagle Hill, Dayview's sister school, since my freshman year. Both programs shared a campus. And a cafeteria. And a student-run coffee shop. "I do art with the kids. They're pretty high-functioning though, different from your group. They just have, like, socialization delays."

"So you draw with them?"

"Sometimes, yeah. We sculpt too. And paint."

"That's really great that you volunteer your time like that."

"It's actually pretty selfish," I insisted. "I like feeling needed."

"I don't believe that."

"You really should," I said with a shrug. "It's true."

We talked about other stuff too—school, kittens, grunge rock ("Pearl Jam's my jam—let's start a nineties tribute band!"), ghosts, colonialism, the REAL meaning of masculinity, and—

"Broken any laws?" I asked.

"Nay. Wait! I voted in the last election."

"Ha. Ever broken curfew?"

"Never."

"Hearts?"

"No way. YOU'RE the heartbreaker," you said to me, shaking your head with a sidelong look. "It's written all over your face."

"Are you flattering me?" I asked, leaning back, daintily sipping the mocha latte you'd bought me. "Because I'm not. I'm always the one that

gets broken."

"You're too beautiful to break."

"Are you for real?" I asked, beaming back, dipping my pinkie into your cappuccino and sucking the foam off my fingertip.

It was the boldest, most flirtatious thing I'd ever done, and you loved it. Your jaw unhinged and your eyes got big—I felt high. Daring and powerful and, honestly, a little incandescent. But then, with that priggish grin of yours that I would come to know so well, you said, "What kind of girl are you?"

And shit, Dan, what kind of question was that? You were smiling like I was in on the joke, so I smiled back, but I should have seen the moment for what it was, should've seen you waving that bright-red flag. I mean, I'd dared to be daring. A little cheeky and coy, and you'd flattened my fizz with your judgment. Of course, I hid my embarrassment for fear of killing the fragile, fledgling spark we'd built. I liked you so much that the thought of losing you, even that early on, felt unbearable. I loved your voice and your hands and your inflections and the way your mouth moved into a round little pout when you said "ooh" sounds. I could envision us kissing and touching and KISSING and TOUCHING, and I felt this immediate and mystifying intimacy with you that, holy hell, completely undid me. What was that? Kismet? Magic? Or just your run-of-the-mill dopamine and adrenaline cocktail?

The walk to Eagle Hill. THE WALK.

Our fingers brushed, and a carbonated current snaked through my body, rushing up my arms and across my chest before slithering back down to my belly button. You were babbling nervously about Hemingway or

Steinbeck—something you were reading/loathing for Lit. I wanted to touch you again, to recreate the sensation I'd felt seconds earlier, but we were stopped now, idling in front the art bungalow, staring at the concrete, not each other.

"Thanks?" I said, chewing my cheeks and twirling my hair. I felt both high and helpless; certain we were soul mates yet scared I'd never see you again.

"For what?" you asked. "For wrecking your uniform?"

I nodded. We watched each other for a long beat.

"You got a phone in that bag?"

"I do." Gleefully, I pulled out my cell, punched in your number, then hit send—kicking the ball back to your court.

"So I'll see you around?"

I'll see you around? I'LL SEE YOU AROUND?! No passionate declarations? No warm kisses or quick, sexy feels? My heart thumped wildly. I resisted the urge to reach out and wreck you; to devour your lips, to maul your hair, to tear off your pressed, plaid button down with my blunt, baby incisors. "Sure," I whispered back, waving as you went. "See you around."

We had a pretty promising start, didn't we, D? Who would've thunk it could've ended like this?

Explosively, devastatingly, calamitously.

Yours truly,

Natalie

I'm a lot of things—a sometimes-liar, an around-the-clock coward, a maybe-cheat. And on really off days like right now, I can be totally miserable. But one thing I'm not is a misogynistic prick. I *loved* that moment at Dayview—her pink fingertip in my coffee, the mischievous glint in her eye—and I hate that she just shit all over it with her warped, dark voodoo, twisting one of the best moments of our relationship into something sinister and black.

But that's what she does. That's her special brand of magic. Taking beautiful things and crushing them.

Herself included.

I crumple up the letter then glance down at the other five that came with it. They're numbered, stacked neatly and bound together with a single satin ribbon. Dramatic, huh? An unexpected morning treat left on my bed like a gift from the fucking fairy of doom. How the hell did she get into my room anyway? Teleportation? Burglary kit? I look left at my busted window, the one that's been wrecked since last spring when she tried breaking in after one of our more explosive fights. It's likely she slipped the package through the permanently cracked space between sill and screen. Clever, Nat. Très creepy.

I grab the notes then follow the soft sounds of percolating coffee to the kitchen. Jessa, my sister, is already up and clanking around in the upstairs bathroom. My dad's gone. Out the door at five every morning, to the gym downtown before work.

I drop a slice of rye bread into the toaster then quickly toss the letters into the oven.

Natalie and her tricks.

She knows today is huge for me. Dayview commencement, the movie's climax. All year I've been following Ryan Espinosa around with my camera, filming his successes and setbacks, documenting every high, every low, every moment with his language and behavioral therapists. Today at five p.m., with twelve other classmates who, at twenty-two, have aged out of the system, he'll don a cap and collect a diploma and eat cake and celebrate. And his mother will cry. And I'll be there digitizing every teardrop.

The toaster dings.

I was a shit boyfriend, true. I tried to please, placate, impress—always falling short. But how do you satisfy someone like Natalie? She's up but down. Hot but cold. Needy and vulnerable yet walled-off and secretive. She's not a girl, she's a riddle. A sexy, scary, manic, messy, inscrutable math problem that I'm done trying to solve.

I crack the oven door; eye her letters with mistrust and suspicion. Do I do it? Do I lift the lid on Pandora's box and read all six of her notes?

I could do without the ridicule, the guilt, the blame and shame for sure, but it's near impossible to pass on an easy opportunity to get her side of the story. Inquiring minds wanna know: Has she found me out? Does she know the real, ugly, untidy truth of it?

I don't even know what to hope for.

DECEMBER 2, 2015, WEDNESDAY, 6:43 P.M., TEXT

From: Dan Jacobson

To: Natalie Fierro

Dan: I can't stop thinking about French Algeria and Eddie Vedder.

Natalie: Liar. Be bold and tell me what's really on your mind.

Dan: The mask of masculinity.

Dan: Okay, YOU.

Natalie: A++. Now ask me out for real.

MAY 19, 2017, FRIDAY, 7:16 A.M., TEXT

From: Ruby Lefèvre

To: Dan Jacobson

We need to talk. ASAP.

JUNE 2, 2016, THURSDAY, CHAT

11:42 p.m. Arielle_Schulman: You're cute. ;)

11:54 p.m. Arielle_Schulman: JK, you're hideous.

12:01 a.m. Arielle_Schulman: Hello . . . ? Dan?

DanWithABattlePlan has signed off.

2

Dear Dan,

Three hints: I'm cold, I'm dizzy, I'm spinning in circles!

Any guesses? Are you loving this roundabout, rickety trip down memory lane?

I'll clue you in: I'm at the playground by the reservoir, setting the scene for a rehashing of date two (though actually, if I'm being technical, this is the location of date one, since Dayview wasn't really a date, was it?). Can you picture it? The swings, the slides, the bumpy asphalt and trampled grass? Today this place is vibrant—bright with purple wisteria and blooming jasmine. But the night we were here it was cold and black. We'd spent that day roaming Silver Lake—sipping cocoa, spilling secrets, selling each other the supersexy versions of our very best selves. I was the adorkable art lover who'd just had a massive collage piece in a teen show at the Getty. You were the documentarian slash socially aware

18

overachiever. We were destined to love each other, don't you think? The star and the saint? The good boy and the artsy kook?

"So, wait." I needed to know everything about you—your aspirations, your fantasies, your dirty secrets and hard-line values. I settled for asking, "How'd you end up working at—"

"My mom was a nurse at Dayview," you finished for me. "She had a thing for kids with, like, developmental delays. She's dead now."

"Oh."

You looked gutted suddenly.

"I'm so sorry," I said, grabbing your hand and squeezing it. "How'd she die?" Pushy, I know, but we were onto something, you and me: a legit connection. Starter love. Why waste time with trite platitudes about death?

"Cancer."

"You okay?"

You shrugged sheepishly. "Do I look okay?"

I inspected you; equal parts boy and man—tall and broad with the face of a marble god. "You're perfect."

Your mouth split into a wide, goofy grin and I suddenly had a new life goal: to make you smile like that every day forever. "So . . . ," you said. "You make collages?"

I clutched my coat to my chest. It was four p.m. and nearly dark; the city was aglow with tiny lights and reflective Christmas decorations. "Right."

"With what? Like, magazine cutouts?"

"Sure, sometimes." The street curved into a small residential pocket. My

feet—which I'd shoved into my cutest, smallest flats that morning—were killing me. "Mostly I do portraits. Girls' faces, made with, like, other girls' faces."

"My brain just exploded."

I smiled. "It's a lot of Xeroxing onto colored construction paper. Can we stop?"

"Talking about collage art?"

"No, I mean, can we stop walking?" I offered no excuses, convinced you'd dismiss me as ridiculous if I even hinted at my love for impractical footwear.

"Yeah, sure." You pointed at a park—THE park; OUR park—just a few yards off. "Know any good games?"

"Hide-and-seek? Or, oh wait—you mean, like, mind games?"

"Here, c'mere," you said, pulling me toward a tot-sized, metal merry-go-round. "Want a ride?"

Hells yeah I did. I grabbed the handlebars and waited to be spun into oblivion. You delivered: turning me around and around. I leaned back, letting my hair go wild while the stars swirled above me.

"Well?" you said, letting the carousel twist on its own for a bit before it wobbled and slowed to a stop. "Had enough?"

"Never."

You held my gaze for what felt like forever.

And then you kissed me.

I don't even know how it happened. I was dazed and exultant from the ride still. Your lips were hot and soft and your hands were everywhere—

my face, my hips, tangled up in my hair. "I like you so much," you whispered into the shoulder of my jacket.

I'd never felt happiness like that before.

"Me too," I said, hooking my chin around your neck. Our bodies clicked into place like plastic dolls built to fit.

It all seemed so fated and right that night, didn't it? Like the gods of the Silver Lake Recreation Center had given us the green light to love each other? Except that now it's been eighteen months, and I've got hindsight on my side. Turns out? This park is just a park. It's sunny and overrun with germy toddlers and frazzled parents. There's no crescent moon now. No sweet kisses or crisp night air. No swirl of stars and possibility.

I'm watching these kids play freeze tag. This tiny guy is chasing down a miniature blond spitfire—sixish with pigtails. She's screaming gleefully and so is he—they're both giddy and jumpy and breathless. That's what it's like, isn't it? The falling-for-someone part? The thrill and anticipation of the chase? Of BEING chased? It's fast and disorienting and insanely fun.

But what happens when you finally catch the girl, huh, Dan? When she's real and right there and she's loving you back?

She's disappointing, isn't she? Too vulnerable and fragile and flawed? So you're like, "Sayonara, girl!" but this is freeze tag, remember? You may have moved on, but Pigtails, she hasn't—she's stuck still, frozen in place; killing herself trying to sort out what she did wrong to make you stop loving her.

Fun sport, huh?

Not for me, Dan. Consider this my official resignation.

I'm dropping out of the game.

Nat

I remember that kiss a little differently.

I remember the lead-up. The time that lapsed between Dayview and the rec center; the anticipation, the nerves, the obsessing and relentless fantasizing. I mean, that kiss—it didn't just *happen*. I texted, I google-stalked, I sent cat pictures that I captioned with pithy, clever one-liners. I wanted her, she's right about that, and if you want to get technical, then yeah, sure, you could call it chasing.

But here's where Nat gets it wrong: I never caught up. Not that night, not later in our relationship, not even during our breakup—because that girl never stops moving. She's impossible to catch. A wild, shifty thing who—let's be clear here—isn't the little toy train she makes herself out to be. She's the Concorde, flying nonstop at supersonic speeds. That's part of what drew me in initially, that unstoppable energy and verve. I wanted to fly alongside her, so yeah, I chased her. But you gotta know when to quit, right? Maybe it's weak. Maybe *I'm* weak. But I just got tired of running.

Two down, four to go. Christ, I still can't keep up.

I tuck the letter back its envelope and quickly check my cell. Another text from Ruby:

CALL ME.

I'm not calling.

I switch off my phone, dump my dishes in the sink, and

head upstairs to shower. Natalie's face flashes in my mind—head tipped back, hair flying. She was so beautiful that night. Happy and free. Maybe I did this all wrong. Took the easy way out. I should have fought harder instead of being the asshole coward who quits when shit gets rough.

I could call her now, come clean; admit my wrongdoing and beg her forgiveness and then maybe, just maybe, we could try again?

Or maybe not.

Because here's the truth: my life these past few weeks—sans Natalie—has been pleasantly serene and drama-free. Our relationship was like that merry-go-round—fast and thrilling but completely dizzying. No matter how many times we went around and around, we always ended up in the same spot. I can't go back to that again. I'm sick of spinning in circles.

"Consider this my official resignation. I'm dropping out of the game."

I stop outside the bathroom door, my mind reeling back to those last lines of her letter. *Dropping out. Official resignation.* What exactly is she hinting at? My immediate impulse is to get in the car and drive to her place—reassure myself that her need for drama hasn't escalated to a darkly sensational place. Sensibly, I stop myself. This—the coded language and thinly veiled threats—it's nothing new. As Ruby would say: "It's classic Nat." She baits me with a good ol' manipulative guilt trip and I go running.

Well, not this time, I'm not falling for it.

I want off the Natalie Fierro thrill ride.

DECEMBER 18, 2015, FRIDAY, 5:33 P.M., EMAIL

From: Alexa McKay

To: Natalie Fierro

Okay, I've stalked him online and you're absolutely right, he's adorable. He looks corn-fed and broish but in a sad, soulful way that works. I hope he worships you, Nat, really truly, because you deserve it, especially after your adventures with what's-his-face and that other awesome A-Hole Who Shall Not Be Named.

BUT.

But!

Dude, I miss you. Can we please hang out this weekend? PLEASE? Pizza? Roller rink? Caffeine-fueled, dollar-store shopping spree? Surely Public School Boyfriend can spare you for one measly night.

XXX,

Lex

DECEMBER 21, 2015, MONDAY, 10:54 P.M., TEXT

From: Natalie Fierro

To: Alexa McKay

Lex, I'm sooo sorry for being a mo-fo no-show! I'm a jerk! Forgive me? I was with the boy and lost track of time . . .

Fluff, Alexa called the landline again. She's still having a hard
time reaching you on the cell. Call back.

P.S. Here's a twenty for takeout. We have Mom's benefit at
Redcat tonight and then tomorrow we're out with the Sobels.

—Dad

3

Novio, I'm in SUCH a mood.

I'm lying here on the floor of my Mod-Podge-splattered studio, feeling desperately, wretchedly nostalgic for our easy early days. Remember what love was like before we destroyed it with our petty and monumental bullshit? I'm talking about the pre-sex days, when every kiss felt flipping epic; when just brushing up against each other was like being zapped by a benevolent stun gun. Remember the first time you came to the studio? I swear to God, Dan, stripping naked for you would've been easier. I was so scared you'd run screaming when you finally saw my collages; saw the fragmented, odd portraits that dressed the cement ceiling and walls. Girls upon girls patched together with pieces of other girls: pretty ones, ugly ones, sleeping ones, dying ones. Long, elegant necks I'd made with feet clipped from shoe catalogs. Big, poufy lips I'd done with nipples cut from porno mags.

"Whoa" was all you said at first. You were standing in the middle of the room doing circles, scanning each portrait with wide, weird eyes.

"You're freaked out," I said definitively, hating myself, wondering how long it would be before you backed out of our relationship. You'd seen my work, you'd seen the real me, and now you were wondering, "Who's this whack job artist I'm dating? What kind of sicko spends her Saturdays doing craft projects with photos of dismembered body parts?"

But, "It's really phenomenal," you were saying instead, zeroing in on my most recent project: a half-done portrait of Lex I'd been working on for weeks. "The textures and the attention to detail. Like, how the hell did you DO this?" I felt a fast and hard rush of relief while you talked on. "The way this girl's cheeks look like they're flushing?"

"That's Alexa," I said quickly. You two were about to meet, remember? She was probably already waiting for us around the block at Wurstküche. "Wait fifteen minutes, and you'll be able to compare the original with the replica."

"The shadows . . ."

"It's nothing special," I said, getting hot now, suddenly high off your praise and approval. "Really, it just takes a long time, finding the right colors to shade with."

You reached for me and pulled me forward in a swift motion that felt like a dance move. "You scare me a little, Fierro."

My stomach bubbled then dropped. Here it was, the moment I'd been dreading: when you finally admitted that you preferred sweet, prudish girls over weirdos who loved decoupage. "I scare you?"

"Yeah," you said, leaning forward, touching my nose with your nose.

Testing the waters, I tilted my chin up: our lips grazed lightly.

"You know, like, your brain," you said inside my mouth.

"What about my brain?" We were kissing suddenly. You were pressing me into a tiny portrait I'd done of Mariella, our housekeeper.

"It's like you got a better one than the rest of us."

My shoulder blades rocked the canvas. "That's not true," I said, because it wasn't. Later you'd learn this. That my mind was a tricky labyrinth made up of dead ends and dark caves.

"It is," you said, cupping my face. "It just IS. You're a star, Nat."

A freaking STAR, Dan. I nearly imploded with glee. What feels better than being told you're the best by the best person you know? "I'm not," I said, demurring, wanting to seem humble and sweet and coolly oblivious, as if it had never even occurred to me to pursue art with any sort of sincere commitment. I pretended not to want the things I wanted—fame, recognition, a future in art—because I thought you'd respect me more if I seemed self-effacing and humble. I loved that you encouraged my interests and talents, and I didn't want to spoil it all by owning up to the truth: that I was, that I AM, shamefully ambitious. That art stardom is something I've been gunning for since I was a kid splashing around in Mae's toxic oil paints. That I have a vision board buried at the back of my closet plastered with photos of Art Basel and the Whitney Biennial. That I am, that I always have been, striving to surpass my mother's success.

"Nat . . ." You were touching me softly now, your fingers tracing my bumpy spine up up up; your lips whispering my name into the hollows *of my collarbone.*

I felt grossly validated and insanely turned on, and I miss that feeling now, Dan. Even on days when I hate you I think of moments like this when I loved you, and I remember that being your girl on good days was better than any high (from any guy) I've ever known.

Fondly,

Natalie

She's mostly right about that night, that's when I really fell for her. Blame it on the paint fumes or the aphrodisiac effects of newsprint and glue, but she really dazzled me with her talent. Nat's studio was as visually stunning as it was assaulting, and had I not known where I was that night I might've thought I was trapped inside the prison cell of a creatively inclined paranoid schizophrenic. Or a genius. Though those two things aren't mutually exclusive, I guess.

I'd known other arty girls before Nat. I'd had friends at school who'd dabbled in ceramics and sculpture, who had taken shitty, shadowy photos that they thought were edgy and avant-garde. For them art was just a hobby. Something they did after school or on weekends that they talked about pursuing in college but likely never would. And not to sound like a complete dick, but I just sort of figured that Nat was the same way. That collaging was a pastime, something she did to blow off artistic steam. Sounds ridiculous, I know, since I'd known about her Getty show, I'd *known* that her mother was a semi-famous painter, but I just hadn't met any girls before Nat that had matched me in talent and drive.

Not only did she match me. She surpassed me.

I hadn't recognized it before, but there it was on a platter: *you're dating a girl who's too good for you, Dan.*

We never did meet up with Alexa that night. We stayed

31

at the studio and did filthy and fantastic things to each other. But when we finally did meet up with her several weeks later, she was nothing like the blushing, shy girl I thought I'd seen in Nat's portrait. She was tall and skinny in a shapeless black dress, waving a menu enthusiastically from the back of the line at Wurstküche. "Hi!"

Nat threw herself at Lex like a lover might. "This is him!" she said, meaning me. She pulled back and pointed. "He's cute, right?"

"He is," Lex said, extending a hand, which I shook. "*Enchanté*, Public School Boyfriend."

"Pleasure," I said, stiffening a little.

"This line is atrocious," Lex said, and it was, it wrapped around the block. "Dan, do you like pizza?"

"You mean sausages?" We were in line for sausages.

"*Pizza*," she repeated with exasperation. "Or hiking? Fly fishing maybe? Installation art?"

I looked at Nat nervously. "What's she doing right now?"

"I'm trying to find some common ground," Lex said to me like *duh*. "Have you ever made pasta from scratch?"

"She's fucking with you," Nat said, squeezing my hand reassuringly. Then to Lex, "Stop fucking with him."

"I'm a pretty big film buff," I offered lightly.

"Oh yeah? Me too. I just saw this old movie . . . *Meshes of the Afternoon*?"

Meshes was a surrealist short made in the forties. No way in hell would anyone our age know it unless they were a complete cinephile. "Oh man, that's a rough one."

"Too esoteric, right?"

"Yeah, just, like, way too trippy."

Her smile relaxed into something softer and more genuine. Nat looked at Lex and then back at me and said, "Awesome, you passed her test with flying colors. Now can we talk about something that I like to talk about?"

"Like what?" Lex said. "Like *you*?"

"Sure, why not," Nat said, smiling impishly while rubbing against Lex like a cat. "Let's talk about me me *me*."

Later, inside, we ate veggie sausages slathered in mustard and relish. Nat and Lex sat together on the other side of the communal table, making in-jokes, throwing food, whispering to each other then laughing loudly because unlike me they just couldn't give two shits about good manners or shame. That's how it is in LA when you're raised by rich, brash, famous people.

Take Lex's dad: a former playboy and drug addict who was in a hugely popular hair band in the eighties before committing successfully to a sober existence as a husband, dad, and music exec. Her mother, an ex-catalog-model, now threw ostentatious parties that somehow raised money for starving children in Africa. Alexa, just like Natalie, could do whatever the hell she wanted in life because her parents had paved her way. She could go to China for a semester (and she had—she now spoke semi-fluent Mandarin). She could pursue a career as an actress (and she was—she'd just booked a small but recurring role on a popular daytime soap.). She could eat caviar-covered truffles with a side of foie gras at every meal. She could behave abysmally in restaurants. Not that she had exactly, but she *could*. I, however, could not.

Because I went to public school.

Because my dad was a tax attorney with mountains of debt.

"Nat says you make movies?" Alexa asked, gazing lovingly at Nat, not me.

"Yeah, nothing feature length yet. I'm working on a documentary short right now about a kid I work with at Dayview."

"Oh, where Nat volunteers. That's how you two met."

"Right."

"So that's the ultimate for you, Dan?" Lex's head was cocked, her tongue resting in the crook between her upper and lower lip. "Documentaries? That's your aspiration?"

It *was* my aspiration. I was *aspiring* still. Unlike these two, who were already making shit happen. How had I not managed to complete a project yet? Why hadn't I shown at Sundance already or SXSW? I sat there grinning dully doing the math: Nat's insane talent coupled with her mother's contacts could really take her far in life. And even if I *could* one day match her in genius and drive, I'd still have to work twice as hard just to keep the pace. Would I ever measure up? If we stayed together long-term would she eventually see through me and lose interest? Did I even deserve her attention now?

"Yep, filmmaker, that's the goal," I said, holding my smile steady. Nat bit the tip off a french fry and beamed back with pride.

R_Lefèvre: You're up.

DanWithABattlePlan: Yeah, just Google-stalking Natalie, no biggie.

R_Lefèvre: Find anything?

DanWithABattlePlan: I'm on Getty Images obsessing over a photo of her from some event last year. She's with a guy. Trying to figure out if they dated.

R_Lefèvre: Can't Google tell you that sort of stuff now?

DanWithABattlePlan: Amazingly, no.

R_Lefèvre: And Getty Images? Who the hell is this girl? A Disney princess?

DanWithABattlePlan: He looks rich.

R_Lefèvre: Are his teeth capped with solid gold?

DanWithABattlePlan: No, but he's wearing a diamond tiara.

R_Lefèvre: Then he probably isn't bonking your girl, Dan.

DanWithABattlePlan: I'm losing my mind.

R_Lefèvre: You're jealous?

DanWithABattlePlan: Violently.

R_Lefèvre: Huh.

DanWithABattlePlan: What?

R_Lefèvre: Nothing.

DanWithABattlePlan: WHAT?

R_Lefèvre: I mean, is she really THAT great?

DanWithABattlePlan: Yes.

R_Lefèvre: Really?

DanWithABattlePlan: Yes.

DanWithABattlePlan: We went out with a friend of hers tonight. Alexa McKay.

R_Lefèvre: Should I know her?

DanWithABattlePlan: She's on a soap opera.

R_Lefèvre: So?

DanWithABattlePlan: So Nat's whole crowd is famous.

R_Lefèvre: I'd hardly call soap stardom the pinnacle of fame.

DanWithABattlePlan: I don't know what's wrong with me.

R_Lefèvre: I don't know what's wrong with you either.

DanWithABattlePlan: I've never liked anyone this much before.

DanWithABattlePlan: Hello?

DanWithABattlePlan: Ruby?

R_Lefèvre: I'm here.

DanWithABattlePlan: You okay?

R_Lefèvre: Why?

DanWithABattlePlan: I don't know.

DanWithABattlePlan: What'd you do earlier?

R_Lefèvre: Veggie sushi night here at the Lefèvre house.

DanWithABattlePlan: Seaweed salad?

R_Lefèvre: You know it.

DanWithABattlePlan: Rubes.

R_Lefèvre: What?

DanWithABattlePlan: I really want you guys to meet.

R_Lefèvre: Mmk.

DanWithABattlePlan: You don't wanna meet her?

R_Lefèvre: No I do.

DanWithABattlePlan: Will you google this guy and tell me he's a troll?

R_Lefèvre: What's his name?

DanWithABattlePlan: Jason Paruch.

R_Lefèvre: He looks smug as shit.

DanWithABattlePlan: Right?

DanWithABattlePlan: Should I be worried?

R_Lefèvre: About?

DanWithABattlePlan: I don't know. Is he better than me?

R_Lefèvre: You're fishing.

R_Lefèvre: No, Dan, no one's better than you.

DanWithABattlePlan: Promise?

R_Lefèvre: Don't be desperate. It's not a good look.

4

Break out the candy hearts and pink carnations, Dan!

It's me again, the Ghost of Love-Gone-Wrong, here to guide you through the memory of our first and only Valentine's together: the Chinese takeout, the sparkling cider, Casablanca on mute, and Django Reinhardt on the stereo . . .

I'm wondering right now if you're wondering if I'm writing you from your dad's basement. After all, that's where we spent the holiday—eating Slippery Shrimp with our fingers, reading Edna St. Vincent Millay poems, kissing and staring and groping and—are you picturing it? Me with my fancy calligraphy pen, crouched under the staircase while you and Jessa make spaghetti upstairs?

Hello, stalker!

Oh relax, boyfriend of yore, I'm not THAT crazy. I'm recreating the moment at home with a bottle of Martinelli's and some frozen Szechuan

Beef.

So, okay, flashback to that night, which started off pretty shitty: I showed up at your place in a mood after wasting the afternoon with my mother—she'd just been commissioned by the Westwood W to do this large-scale Picasso knockoff for their newly renovated lobby, and she had spent the better part of that week living out of her studio while I stayed home eating organic pop tarts with Mariella, my real mom. Dad, the parent who usually doles out the cash, was in Korea for work, so I asked my mother for money. I needed a little extra for your V-day gift, and, if I'm being completely frank, I just sort of felt like taking something from her. If she wasn't going to give me love and hot, home-cooked meals, then the least she could do was make up for it with cold hard cash.

"I'm not giving you money," she said, readjusting her paint-splattered smock. "Dad gave you two hundred bucks before he left—what the hell did you spend it on?"

"I needed to feed myself."

"Oh please, Natalie, I stocked the fridge Sunday night."

"I don't like what you bought."

"Tough shit."

"I've been ordering rolls from Katsu-Ya."

Her head snapped around, eyes huge. "All week?"

"All week."

"That's exorbitant."

That was the point.

"Please?" I pleaded. "It's Valentine's."

You were on a David Foster Wallace kick back then, remember? There was this signed, first edition copy of *Infinite Jest* for sale at the Last Bookstore downtown. I wanted to buy it for you.

"I need to get Dan something."

"Well, Fluff, you should've thought of that before you blew two hundred bucks on spicy tuna rolls." She scrunched her eyes and slapped the canvas with a messy blob of orange paint. And that was the end of that.

So I showed up at your house empty handed. And I was mortified, remember? A spoiled brat who'd eaten her weight in gilded ginger while her boyfriend went gift-less on the most romantic day of the year.

"I'm an asshole," I said to you as you stripped off my coat and nuzzled your nose in my neck. "Don't give me anything, I don't deserve it."

"What about kisses?"

"Unearned!" I wailed, but you kissed me anyways. You were always doing things like that—loving me when I didn't deserve to be loved.

"Come with me," you said, pulling me down the hall and down the stairs and down down down to the basement, which you'd decorated with—from the looks of it—zero restraint. There were drippy candles in chianti bottles, heart-shaped boxes of chocolates, pink roses, red balloons, and all the stock symbols of romance.

I looked at you, speechless. "This is . . ."

"What?"

"It's . . ."

"Foul, say it."

"Yeah," I said, laughing. "It's absolutely nauseating."

You grinned and kissed me again. It was a slow one this time, soft and electric.

"Do you think I'm a terrible person for trying to extort large sums of money from my mother?" I asked.

"How large?"

"Triple digits."

"What do you need that kind of cash for? Clothes?"

"I want to buy you things."

You smiled and shrugged me off. "You don't have to do that."

"But I want to."

"But you don't work."

I jolted backward, stung. "So?"

"So, you shouldn't be spending that kind of cash then."

My chest tightened. "You think you're better than me because you work? You think I'm just some vapid, privileged bitch who sits around all day fucking fanning herself while trolling the internet for expensive shoes?"

"Whoa, Nat." You scooped me up in your arms and cradled me while I got teary. "Whoa, no. NO. I think you're incredible. You're smart, you're weird, you make awesomely messed-up art—" I laughed at that and let you squeeze me tighter. "I just mean—don't spend your parents' money on me. That's it."

I sat up, sniffling, looking you square in the eye. "It's true, though. I'm a brat. You should've seen me with my mother earlier . . ." I shook my head, abashed. "Is it normal to hate your parents that much?"

You blinked. You didn't say anything back, so I said, "What, you hate *me now?"*

"Stop it, seriously. I love everything about you."

I love everything about you.

I LOVE everything about you.

Exhilaration shot from my head to my heart. It was nearly an "I love you," wasn't it? A pre "I love you"? I let it roll around inside my body for a bit. "Everything?" I asked greedily, grabbing you, nipping at your earlobe like a hungry baby animal.

"Everything," you whispered back, wiping my tear-streaked face. "I never want to be the reason you cry. I will never, ever hurt you, Nat. Not ever."

LIES.

LIESLIESLIESLIESLIES.

You did hurt me, Dan.

And you're still doing it.

Nat

These past few weeks, the post-break-up weeks, I've been driving around on autopilot—feeling sad but in a manageable way: regretful, yes, wistful at times, sure, but mostly I've just been bouncing back and forth between mild guilt and massive relief. No more fights with Nat; no more tears or tantrums. I've reinvested in school and re-committed myself to the movie. Life's been okay.

Until this morning. And shit, I should've known. What the hell was I expecting? That Nat and I would part ways amicably? That we'd keep in touch via social media? See each other twice a year for coffee catch-ups? Send each other postcards from our respective sides of the city?

Hell no.

It's Natalie.

Natalie.

She's batshit and brilliant and even though this relationship retrospective of hers has been relatively tame thus far, I know there's something larger lurking in the distance. She's got a 10K fireworks display hiding behind a curtain where she's crouched with a box of matches, twirling her mustache.

I shove the note in my equipment bag and glance out the window at the desolate stretch of San Fernando speeding by. I've been doing this commute every weekday for the past three years—Metrolink from downtown to North Hollywood and back. It's exhausting. But Nat used to make it tolerable. She'd meet me most days after school at Union Station. Wait on the outdoor train platform in her uniform—bobby socks and bright-red lipstick—grinning while the Santa Anas whipped her hair wildly from side to side; sun setting behind the mountains; eighties metal blaring in surround sound.

"Snacks," she said to me one afternoon early on in our relationship, thrusting a white paper bag into my hands as we exited the station and headed for her car. "There's some chips in there, some dried fruit, some other stuff—to tide you over till dinner."

"You're incredible."

"I'm pragmatic," she said. "You're always ravenous."

I reached into the bag and pulled out a giant, lumpy cookie. "Oh man." I took a bite, dying a little. It was fantastic—subtly sweet and buttery with bitter chocolate. "Jesus."

"Right?" She smiled knowingly. "They're from a bakery on Larchmont."

"Are you an angel?" I asked, devouring the rest in two quick chews.

"Don't you know yet?" She shimmied her shoulders. "I'm the devil."

We zigzagged across the lot to Nat's old Buick Riviera—tan exterior, gray interior—lots of rich, arty girls on the Eastside drive junk cars. "What're we doing for dinner?"

"What do you feel like?" I asked, getting in. Scrambling to come up with cheap options. "Guisados? Or burgers maybe?"

"Can we go to your house instead? Make frozen pizzas?" She looked at me pleadingly. Nat loved my house. She was always saying things like, "It feels so homey and authentic here," and "You have, like, an actual *den*. With *carpet*." Her parents' place was distressingly modern—all hard angles with glass and concrete.

So we went to my house. We made boxed macaroni and cheese with small sides of frozen broccoli. Dad stayed in his study working on a brief, and Jessa and her friend—a quiet girl with a face full of makeup—hung out on the front deck filming themselves with my camera. "That chick has five hundred thousand subscribers on YouTube," Nat whispered to me over a forkful of broccoli. "I've seen her videos. She has, like, a whole tutorial on how to make lipstick with powdered Kool-Aid."

We watched a movie after that. Something Nat wanted to watch; something frothy and romantic which was fine because Nat had her feet in my lap—dainty things painted with glossy pink polish. She was squirming and smiling; cringing gleefully while the people on TV fell in and out of love.

"Could you ever love anyone like that?" she asked a little later as the film score picked up; rain and tears melting makeup off the faces of the lovelorn leads.

I laughed. I knew what she was really asking: *Could you ever love ME like that?*

And I could. I would.

Instead I shrugged and said, "Maybe," and she crawled into my lap; a slow, wobbly creep like a cat or a baby or a seductress.

"I don't want to go home tonight," she said.

"So don't."

We kissed and she shivered a little.

"You okay?" I asked, rubbing her arms and pulling her close. "You cold?"

"No, I'm just—" Her eyes were suddenly wet. "I'm just really, really happy that I'm with you."

It was such a small moment—it wasn't Valentine's or The Park or Dayview—but it was Nat at her best: earnest, sweet, a little vulnerable.

I think about that night a lot. Everything felt so regular and right then. So much promise and possibility. So little disappointment and doubt. That's the version of Nat I miss most now: the unguarded girl who liked wall-to-wall carpeting. The one who trembled when we kissed late at night. The one who ate boxed mac and cheese like it was fucking filet mignon. Where'd that girl go, huh? The one on the train platform, hair flying everywhere?

The train lurches forward now, jerking me back to reality. I shake off the memory and then quickly glance out the window at the stretch of valley speeding by: strip malls and stopped traffic; juice carts and palm trees. There's the 7-Eleven at the corner of Lankershim and Magnolia—I'm nearly at my stop.

I shove the letter into the front pocket of my backpack and pull out the next in the series, number five: heavy card stock, calligraphic script.

I slip my finger under the envelope flap.

Dan,

Clean up your shit, please. The basement looks like it's been hit by a cartoon-heart missile. It's like Cupid and Casanova had a whole big fuckfest with a bunch of stuffed animals. What the hell were you two doing down there anyways? Wait, don't answer that. Love is disgusting.

Audra's coming over today, and we need the basement to shoot. Have all your crap out by 4:00 p.m.

Thanks!

Jessa

From: Mae Fierro

To: Natalie Fierro

Child o' mine, I had two twenties in my wallet yesterday that have somehow mysteriously disappeared. Did you take them, you little thief???

5

Hi,

I'm back at the park—OUR park—the sacred spot where we shared that explosive/exhilarating/intoxicating first kiss. Though now I'm writing about a different first. A less fun first. My first black eye. Cue the violins. We'd been drinking that night, remember? Whiskey, the good stuff, stolen from my parents' not-so-secret stash. I suggested we go to the park, and you liked the idea, so we went. We took the shortest route—through the hills, down curly streets cluttered with pale-pink houses, down two separate sets of hidden staircases. We got our hair caught in overgrown wisteria vines. We slow-danced to a rap song with a droning drumbeat pumping out the windows of a passing SUV. Twice, you backed me into trees and kissed me like it mattered—pressing against me with your hips and pulling at my hair until it hurt.

"Last one to the swings," I said when we'd finally hit Silver Lake

Boulevard. I was already darting through traffic—yelling and weaving like a drunk idiot.

"Are you crazy?!" you shouted, chasing after me, nearly getting hit yourself; cars swerving behind you, drivers honking and screaming out windows.

"Am I crazy?" We were safe now, panting and grinning; standing at the park perimeter. "Yes! Don't you know that yet?" I meant it as a joke but it came out sounding flat. You stared back at me, head cocked, eyes blinking—as if seeing me for the very first time "What, no cute quip?" I said, and you swatted at me. I ducked, laughed, and ran toward the swing set. "You up for a challenge?"

"What's at stake? Money? Favors?"

"Don't care," I said, meaning it. I didn't give two shits about the prize, I only wanted to win. You grabbed the chains of the neighboring swing, and we both got to work pumping quickly. Within seconds we were neck to neck, flying high; jackets blown open, cheeks flushing pink.

"Look who's ahead now?" you said not too long later. I was losing, which I hated, so I feigned exhaustion and leapt from my swing. But instead of the perfect dismount I'd envisioned—complete with cute curtsy and a wave to the crowd—I botched the landing and fell face-first into a massive, broken branch. "Shit!" That initial jolt of pain was excruciating, like stubbing a toe or getting a hand caught in a doorjamb. I clutched my eye protectively, rocking around in an effort to shake off the ache.

"Jesus, Nat, let me see." You were crouched at my side suddenly, prying my hands away from my throbbing face. "Oh, Nat."

"Is it terrible? Am I deformed?"

"No, it's just—"You laughed, and I relaxed a little, suddenly embarrassed by my hysteria. "It's just red." You kissed it—"You're still gorgeous, Gorgeous"—and then you kissed ME. And then you picked me up and dusted me off and walked me back up the hill to my house.

The next morning I looked like I'd been whacked in the face with a boom mic.

"What the hell happened to you?" my mother said, greeting me with uncharacteristic concern as I shuffled into the kitchen in search of coffee and an ice pack.

"It's fine, it's just a bruise. Dan and I were at the playground last night and I fell off a swing."

"You fell off a SWING?" She inspected my eye, touching it gingerly. "I'm calling Ginsberg."

"I don't need a doctor."

"Have you looked at yourself in the mirror lately?"

I had. I looked horrific.

So I went to see Ginsburg. And whatever, I was fine; you already know how this story shakes out. But here's the noteworthy part—no one questioned the swing bit. Not my mother, not my dad, not even my goddamn pediatrician. I've seen the TV shows: girl shows up with a big, black shiner and it's never an accident, it's ALWAYS the boyfriend. But when the boyfriend is Dan Jacobson—teen heartthrob, good Samaritan— nobody bats a flipping eyelash. Everyone just assumed I was dating a goddamn saint. And who can blame them? I thought that too.

Two days later, when the bruises had ripened into a pretty little constellation of pink and blue stars, I took photos. I thought maybe I'd use the pictures to do some sort of gnarly self-portrait—something provocative and affecting that might earn me some legit art cred. But then I got distracted. My face healed up, I got busy with school, I got busy with you, and eventually I just forgot the whole thing had ever happened.

Until this week, that is, when I dragged all five photos to my desktop and stuck them in a folder titled "Why?"

I wonder if people will ask questions about you now, Dan.

X, Nat

Holy shit, is that what these notes are about? They're part of some larger plot to make me look like a rageful prick? I mean, what're we talking here? Assault charges? Domestic abuse?

God, she's fucking insane. I have never, *ever* laid a hand on her. Whatever psychotic scheme she's hatched, whatever ugly manipulation she's dreamed up—she sure as shit better not see it through because this could easily, *easily* wreck my life.

But she knows that, though, doesn't she? That's her whole MO—play hard, play fast, get dirty.

Last spring, Nat called me shit-faced from a party in West LA: "I need you to come get me," she said, slurring her words. "I'm at Krystal Wang's place in Brentwood and I drank a whole bottle of Two Buck Chuck."

I'd just gotten home from shooting an Espinosa family dinner in Glendale and Jessa still had the car. Annoyed, I nearly told Nat to Uber home but stopped myself. We'd already gone ten days without seeing each other because: "You've been working nonstop, Dan. Don't you care about our relationship? Why don't you miss me as much as I miss you?"

So I went.

It took me an hour and forty-five minutes to get to her by bus, and when I finally arrived—sweaty, irritated, spent—she was passed out in a drained, defunct Jacuzzi in Krystal's packed backyard. "Hey," I said, shaking her. She barely stirred. Her hair was matted to her flushed face and she'd wriggled halfway out of her sundress. "Nat, wake up." I rooted around in her purse—a leather pouch I'd found lying in a small pool of booze at the bottom of the tub. "Where'd you park?"

"Hmm?"

"Your car." I jangled her keys. "Where's it at?"

She cracked one eye. "I thought you were shooting?"

I scooped her up, tossed her over one shoulder—"Come on, sleepyhead"—and carried her around the side of the house, weaving between clusters of kids holding beer bottles and Ping-Pong paddles and Solo cups and cigarettes.

The following morning, after a night spent holding Nat's hair back while she puked in the downstairs half-bath, I drove her home.

"You should've been at that party," she said, yawning, sliding a lazy hand up my thigh toward my crotch.

"Stop, please." I was trying to merge from the 10 to the 110—a tricky intersection that always made me tense.

"Fine." She retreated, pulling her hand back. "How'd the dinner go?"

I smiled, remembering Ryan happily gobbling up small bites of cold cheese tamale with his fingertips. Ryan's dad talking animatedly about the Clippers game. The hibiscus-flavored iced tea. The hour-long interview with Ryan's mom on the deck. "It was really great and, like, pretty moving, you know? They're an incredible family. So warm and funny. They're just, like, trying really hard to make the best of their situation. It's really inspiring."

I looked over. Nat's face was pancake-flat.

"Are you listening?"

"Are you kidding?"

"I'm dead serious. I'm talking about something that's really important to me right now and you couldn't seem *less* engaged."

"I mean, when are you *not* talking about your goddamn movie?"

Stunned, I stuttered a bit before saying, "Are you being serious right now?"

"Oh completely."

"You know how important this project is, right?"

"Yeah, you never let me forget it."

"These kids—"

"I know, I know, they're incredible and you're their mouthpiece. You're doing *such* important work, Dan."

My face flushed with mad heat. Lately I felt like I was working this hard *for her*. To impress *her*. To keep up with *her*, and, "Nat—"

"You know . . ." She rubbed her eyes with two fists, smearing makeup—heavy and black—across her pale cheeks. "If you had come with me last night, I wouldn't have gotten so messed up." She rolled down her window and the air hit my face fast and hard, like a slap. Abruptly, with zero hesitation, she hoisted herself up, thrusting the upper half of her body outside.

Scared shitless, I jumped and the car lurched right. We were doing eighty on the 110, surrounded on all sides; I couldn't slow down or stop or—

"Jesus, Natalie!" I tried dragging her backward by the dress hem, but she resisted, screaming gleefully; waving one hand high in the air while the other clung to the car's interior. "Nat, please! You're scaring me!" My heart was galloping. I was sweating and near tears, reaching for her while trying to keep the car steady.

"You're missing out, Dan!"

I swerved right, laying into the horn, whispering a silent prayer as I tried to get us safely to the freeway shoulder. Nat was waving to fellow motorists while I slammed brakes and accelerated like a lunatic. It was nearly a minute before I reached the emergency lane—finally able to park the car and kill the engine. Nat—eyes wild, hair huge—slunk down in her seat, looking electrified. "That was awesome," she said, breathless and grinning.

"*Awesome*?" My body pulsated with rage. "See this?" I held a hand up; I was trembling still, my fingers shaking with crazy adrenaline. "You fucking terrify me."

Her face changed then—a sudden shift from light to dark.

"I thought you'd appreciate a solid cinematic moment. Where's your camera, Dan?"

It took me a second, but then it dawned on me: she was jealous. Of my movie. "This is about Dayview? Seriously?"

"You *never* make time for me."

"You nearly got us killed just now, you realize that, right?"

"I don't care," she said, pitching forward in her seat, her eyes filling with angry tears. "I'm not afraid to die."

A chill shot through me. "Don't say that."

She looked at me, her chin quivering. "Would you even care?"

"If you *died*? Stop it." Softening, I slid a hand around her head and pulled her close. She let out a broken sob and scurried quickly across the seat, wrapping her arms around my waist like a needy toddler. "You can't do things like that," I said, squeezing her.

"I know. I won't do it again."

"Promise me."

She pulled back, her gaze severe and unblinking. "Swear it," she said, leaning in, sealing the pledge with a kiss.

M_Haney: Were you at Krystal Wang's last night?

Audra_Rey: Yep.

M_Haney: I heard Fierro got shit faced and hit on Bryce De Vitis.

Audra_Rey: She did. Pretty depressing because Jacobson doesn't deserve to be dating a lying skank.

M_Haney: Oh right, she dates Jessa's brother. That's the guy you're in love with.

Audra_Rey: I'm not in love with him. I just think that one day when I'm all grown up he might actually see me and want to marry me and give me babies. He's making a documentary about disabled kids, you know.

M_Haney: Noble. You should blow him.

Audra_Rey: I will one day. I'm just waiting for that romance to implode on its own before I strike.

6

Dan,

If I'm being completely honest (and I am), I've never understood your obsession with Ruby Lefèvre. She's neurotic, she's bitchy, she lacks ambition, and her clothes are drab. If I went to public school and got to wear a brand-new outfit each day, Jesus Christ, I'd make it count: it'd be caftans and miniskirts and moto jackets all year long! And sometimes all at once!

I'm writing you from a bench by Angels Flight ("The Shortest Railway in the World!") and across the street from La Cita, the restaurant where we celebrated Ruby's seventeenth. You were in such a ridiculous mood that night: giddy, jumpy, excited to introduce your "two favorite girls" to each other.

"Rubes, this is Nat."

I was initially thrown by how pretty she was—curvy and fresh-faced;

freckled with big lips. She looked mixed race to me. Half black, half white, maybe? I might've been jealous if her posture had been better. She just looked so . . . defeated.

"Ruby!" I threw myself at her.

"Heyyyyyy," she said, giving me a stiff, one-armed hug. "Great to finally meet you." That was a lie, wasn't it? She looked like she'd just sucked down a liter of lemon juice. "Do you two need drinks? Whitman's brother is bartending. He'll serve you, no questions asked."

"Whitman's brother?"

"Whitman," you said, pointing at an absurdly tall dude standing near us in a ski cap, and then, "Whitman's brother." This was a different guy now, one with longer hair, tending bar. "You want a beer?"

I nodded. I was excited to get some alone time with Ruby. THE Ruby. Your BFF, your partner in crime, the girl with the wicked sense of humor and the sensible sensibility. I tried engaging her, but she was already chatting with a big bunch of Valley dorks. Nerdy girls who wore their smarts as accessories—one girl in a Moby Dick T-shirt, the "K" in the "Dick" stretched widely across her left boob.

"Udon, not ramen," said the boob girl. I was hovering on the periphery of their conversation, stupidly eager to join in.

"I can't do either," said someone else. "They're both wheat."

"They're rice noodles."

"They're not."

"You could eat soba," I said, smiling at the group. "It's made with buckwheat, which is actually, like, a seed."

"A seed?"

"Right, like, quinoa? It's really delicious."

"Who ARE you?" said someone short.

"I'm Natalie."

"Dan's girlfriend," Ruby offered flatly.

"Oooohhh," the girls said back, looking me up then down like judgmental shrews.

Feeling unwelcome, I excused myself; I figured I'd find you by the bar. I'd say, "Ruby's friends suck, let's leave." You'd think I was being intolerant. I'd go, "Dan, it's a girl thing. It's all very subtle." Of course, none of that happened because I couldn't find you—you weren't by the bar or by the bathrooms; you weren't with Whitman on the dance floor. Turns out you were outside on the smoking patio, clutching two wet Tecate cans and talking to a very pretty blonde.

"Who's this?" I said, sidling up.

"Nat, this is Arielle."

"Arielle, huh?" Her dress was tight; her hair, long; her features, sharp and elven, like something out of a Tolkien novel. "How do you know my boyfriend?"

"We have, ah, ceramics together."

"You take, ah, ceramics now?"

"Yeah, since January," you said. "We're making bowls."

"Bowls, huh?"

"And mugs," she said.

"That's cool," I said, trying REALLY HARD to feel cool about it. "I *was thinking of ordering something. You hungry?"*

"Not really." You turned away from me and smiled obliviously at the elf.

"Do you think Turner's single?"

"Turner?" I asked, trying to keep up.

"Our teacher," said the girl. "She's like . . ." She looked at you and laughed, and you laughed back and went, "You kind of have to know her to get it."

"So it's like a private joke," I said.

"Right," said the girl.

"Between you two."

She shrugged. I glared at you. I was THIS CLOSE to implosion. "Can we go, please?"

"We just got here."

"Right, well, Ruby hates me and her friends are bitches, and I didn't come here to stand alone in a corner while you discuss kilns and glazes with—" I shot an expectant look at the blonde.

"Arielle."

"Right, Arielle."

You thrust a Tecate can into my hand and pulled me off to one side. "What's your problem?"

"Nothing. I'm totally cool with you batting your lashes at your ceramics partner while your friends make me feel like a leper."

"I'm not interested in Arielle, Nat. And anyways, she's dating Whitman."

"Oh, but if she were single . . . ?"

"Come on!"

"I want to leave."

"Why?"

"Because you're making me feel like dog shit." I tossed the beer into a trash can and headed back inside.

"Nat!"

"Arielle can drive you home."

"Natalie!"

"What?" I whipped around, livid. "You don't need me. You're surrounded by people who think you're a fucking Adonis."

"Are you for real?"

A nauseating wave of regret hit me like a Mack Truck. Why was I being like this? Had you really given me reason to freak out? Maybe the elf WAS just some girl you glazed bowls with. Maybe Ruby was shy and introverted, not cold and exclusionary. Why was I acting like a needy, petulant six-year-old? "I'm sorry," I whispered, meaning it.

You deflated. "Why don't you trust me?"

"I don't know."

"I don't like Arielle, Nat." You slipped an arm around my waist and pulled me close. "I like YOU."

"Are you sure?" I said, suddenly racked with guilt. How could you like me when I was behaving so badly?

"Yes."

We kissed. It was soft, sweet, and brief. "Ruby hates me."

"She doesn't, she's just not effusive like you." You brushed a few stray hairs from my face. "That temper, Nat . . ."

"I know."

Another kiss. "One beer, okay? Then we'll go?"

"Dan . . ."

"We can't leave yet. It's her birthday, and she's my best friend."

So we stayed.

But I still made you leave after one beer.

Because the drinks didn't make Ruby any nicer, and they certainly didn't make that girl go away.

Nat

Wait, that's it? The sixth and final letter but no explosive finale? No sharp turns or dark twists? *Where's the big blowout, Nat? The fireworks display?*

I get off the train at North Hollywood and start the half-mile trek to school. It's cool out and a little damp—morning dew in the desert. I've plotted this day a billion times before in my head: what I'd need for the after-school ceremony (camera, tripod, tie and blazer), what I'd want to be thinking about (interview subjects to shoot for, questions to ask, list of b-roll shots to get), what I'd need to keep myself panic-free (a mantra, a copy of *Siddhartha*, a Xanax Nat gave me months ago that I keep as a backup just in case the mantra doesn't work). Bottom line: I was prepared for any hiccups in my plan. *Any.*

Except this one.

Instead of worrying about my equipment malfunctioning or my subjects being evasive or boring, I'm wrapped up in some elaborate manipulation designed by my scary, scorned ex-girl-friend. Crazy fluke? Kooky twist of fate? Or exactly what she planned?

That night with Nat was horrible. Her version makes her sound semi-sane, but she went full-blown berserk—scream-ing at me in front of Arielle Schulman, dragging me home almost immediately because of some insignificant, imaginary slight. I spent the following day doing damage control: sending apologies to Arielle and Whitman; trying to get ahold of Ruby, who was ignoring my incessant texts. I ended up having to make amends to Ruby in person; showing up on her doorstep with a spray of purple weeds I'd clipped from my neighbor's backyard.

"What's that?" Ruby asked, folding her arms across her chest and leaning against the stucco exterior of her parents' house. "A 'my girlfriend's an asshole, please forgive me' bouquet?"

"She's not, Rubes, she's just . . ." I searched for the word, but Ruby was right. Nat had been an absolute asshole. "Insecure."

"That's what that is?"

"Be mad at me, okay? Not her?"

"I *am* mad at you. You left."

"Can I come in? Can we talk about it?"

She rolled her eyes and grabbed the weeds. I followed her quickly inside.

Ruby and I met when we were thirteen in an eighth grade language arts class. I'd known she existed before that but barely: she was just another face in the hallway; the quiet girl who stood behind me in the lunch line sometimes; the girl who hung out with Lisa Hicks, the track team's star sprinter.

But Ruby wasn't the star of anything. She wasn't the prettiest or the loudest or the most dramatic or athletic—she wasn't anything really until one day she was everything.

Our spark started small, with some in-class sass about *The*

Old Man and the Sea: "Did I really just waste three days of my life reading about some old dude and a fish?" I'd felt the same way about the book but never would've bashed Hemingway publicly, especially not to our teacher, Krasinski, who had a habit of publicly shaming her more free-thinking students.

I smiled at Ruby. An under-the-radar kind of grin while Krasinski shouted things like "Pulitzer" and "classic" and "your generation." And Ruby smiled back. She reminded me so much of Jessa—all that snark and strength and righteous indignation. She immediately felt like home.

"You got a vase for those things?" I asked as Ruby hurried down the hall to the kitchen. The flowers slapped against her thigh while she walked, tiny petals littering the hardwood floors.

"I think so, yeah. You want tea?"

"Sure, Grandma."

"Don't call me that," she snapped, dropping the weeds into a tall, slender pitcher. Ruby hated—*still* hates—being teased for her pragmatism and maturity. "I'm not your granny."

I winced with guilt. Things had been off with us lately, but pre-Nat, Ruby and I had been so in sync: dirty jokes over sloppy bowls of pho, night hikes in Griffith Park, movie marathons, eating contests, backyard relays with Ruby's kid brother, Noah. "I'm sorry."

"For which part?" she said, her baby face scrunched into

a defensive little grimace. "The part where *you* made me feel insignificant? Or your girlfriend did?"

"See?" I threw my hands up, smiling to undercut the weirdness. "This is all just a big misunderstanding. Nat feels the exact same way, but you're both, like, so important to me."

"I've barely seen you in months."

"You see me every day."

"Yeah, at school." She smiled cheerlessly. "It's not the same."

It wasn't the same; she was right. The week before I met Nat, Ruby had spent three nights at my place in my bed. Nothing sexual of course, things had never gotten romantic between us, but Ruby and I, we liked our sleepovers. We'd make massive plates of linguine with pesto and chase those down with gelato from the fancy Italian place on Vermont. We'd scour Netflix for the most abstruse, esoteric French films we could find, then online stalk the people we hated most. We'd watch acrobatic porn while crying with laughter. We'd get arty and weird together, reading Keats and Plath and Neruda out loud. Occasionally we'd even cuddle, but it was never *a thing*, you know? It was just something sweet that we did that felt really nice—falling asleep, bodies stuffed with foreign foods, limbs warm and loose and entwined. Just some good old-fashioned, harmless fun, though nothing you could do with a girlfriend around. Especially one like Natalie, with a jealous streak as hot and long as a comet tail.

"You're different with her." Ruby was glaring at me now. My heart pinged and I closed the space between us.

"I'm not," I said, going in for a hug. She felt like a slab of cement. "You're not letting me fix this."

"I don't know what you want me to say," she said, pulling back, the crinkle between her brow deepening. "I don't like her."

"You don't know her."

"Regan Weiss does. She says she's completely psychotic."

"Stop it."

"And Whitman said she had a full-blown meltdown on the smoking patio last night."

"It wasn't a meltdown!" I said, even though it was totally, irrefutably a meltdown. "She felt threatened."

"By *what*?"

"She thought Arielle—"

"Let me guess." Ruby shook her head, cutting me off. "She thinks she's into you."

"She does, but—"

"Oh come on, you're gonna try and deny it? She's like a salivating puppy around you!"

I felt both flattered and freaking afraid.

"Promise me something."

"What?"

"That you'll be careful around her."

"Arielle?"

"No, dork. Your crazy girlfriend."

I exhaled dramatically. "Can you give her a chance? Please?"

Ruby watched me for a long beat; eyes like slits. "Why do you like her?"

I didn't answer. Something red and angry was bubbling up from my stomach.

"I just don't think she's good for you, Dan."

"But she is."

Ruby's face was purple. She took a breath, locking eyes with me. "Are you sure about that?"

Was I?

"You're playing with, like, nuclear explosives," Ruby said. "You realize that, right?"

"Is that a metaphor?"

"I'm trying to protect you."

"I don't need protection."

"Have you slept with her yet?"

My face got hot. We hadn't, we were virgins still. Nat had wanted to wait until the moment felt "exactly right." "Does it matter?"

"Well, if you're having sex, you're screwed. Pun intended." She punched my arm lightly then cracked a smile. "Otherwise, you can still get out of the relationship fairly unscathed. Girls get, like, super attached when they sleep with a guy." She shrugged awkwardly. "I would imagine guys do too?"

"Ruby." Why wasn't she getting this? "I don't. Want. Out."

She flinched a little, looked down quickly—"Fine"—and then fingered a few of the purple petals that had fallen onto the marble countertop. "Just don't come crying to me when she boils your bunny."

"Huh?"

"Fatal Attraction, bud." She slammed the kettle onto the stovetop and cranked the gas to high. "Look it up."

MARCH 20, 2016, SUNDAY, 6:54 P.M., TEXT

From: Unknown Number

To: Dan Jacobson

Hope I didn't make too many waves last night for you and your

girl. I'm a troublemaker. ;) Apologies. X, Ari

**MARCH 20, 2016, SUNDAY, SCRAP PAPER NOTE TACKED TO DAN'S DAD'S
CAR WINDSHIELD**

PETE,

LESLIE SAW DAN ROOTING AROUND IN THE FLOWERS

THIS MORNING PICKING ALL OF OUR LAVENDER. NEW

GIRLFRIEND? I'M ALL FOR ROMANCE, BUT FOR THE

LOVE OF GARDENING, CAN YOU PLEASE KEEP YOUR

KID OFF OUR LAWN?

DAVID

**MARCH 21, 2016, MONDAY, DVD COPY OF FATAL ATTRACTION STUCK
INSIDE THE SLATS OF DAN'S LOCKER; WITH IT, A STICKY NOTE THAT
READS:**

Watch and weep.

—R

7

DAN, 8:57 A.M.

Last year around Christmastime, Nat was helping out after
school at Eagle Hill—stringing popcorn and cranberries with
the kids, making construction paper wreaths and felt stockings;
baking cookies, being cheery, being the best version of Nat. I
was across campus at Dayview with Ryan doing similar stuff,
only I was filming it and I was struggling. Trying to get him to
meet one of his functional reading goals—to identify an item,
just one, on his multiple choice task cards. He'd done it before,
but now that I was filming he was refusing—smiling, rocking,
shaking then hiding his head. He'd even snubbed my cookie
bribes—broken pieces of crispy gingerbread from the Dayview
café. So I'd gone to get Nat. Because she was great with the
kids, sure, but also because she was just so skilled at persuading
people to do the things that they didn't want to do.

"Can I borrow you for a minute?" I asked, poking my head inside her classroom. Kids were everywhere being cute maniacs—eating, singing, crafting, farting. Nat was on the floor with a small brown-haired boy, the two of them hip to hip wielding scissors; Nat making something complicated with cardboard, the boy tracing the outline of a snowflake with his finger.

"What can I do you for?" she said, looking up.

"Can you help me with Espinosa?"

"Right now?"

"Twenty minutes tops, I swear. I'm just trying to get some footage of him reading."

She faced the boy and pushed some hair off his forehead. "What do you think, buddy? Can you spare me for a bit?" He smiled broadly, his two front teeth missing.

We spent nearly an hour in the senior bungalow—me hovering with my camera while Nat and Ryan ate M&Ms and played Jenga. They drew dolphins together. They drew rainbows. Nat said, "Screw task cards!" And found a clever backdoor way for Ryan to meet his goals—by rewarding him with huge hugs every time he was able to identify an object she'd drawn.

Watching them together like that—even rewatching the footage later on? It broke my heart in the very best way.

"Dan?"

Cohen's hovering over me, waving around a ripped copy of

Gilgamesh.

"Sorry?"

"Your thoughts on Gilgamesh and Enkidu's relationship: platonic? Romantic?"

"I—" I haven't read a word of it. I scan the room for an ally, but all I see are bored, blank faces.

"Dan." Cohen drops her arm and the book smacks against her bony hip. "Do your homework."

The bell dings. I grab my crap, hang my head low, then scuttle out into the packed hallway where I immediately slam into Whitman and this other guy, Will Brizendine. "Jacobson!" They slap my shoulders and hands, grinning broadly. "How's it going?"

I slap back, my eyes darting left. There's Arielle, avoiding my gaze, clinging to Whitman's arm like a shy child. I mumble something about pre-calc and dart off.

Seconds later, when I'm only a few feet away from my locker, I see it: the cream-colored edges poking out the slats of my metal cubby; the red ribbon taunting me like a mischievous snake. The calligraphy. The heavy cardstock. It's another package from Nat.

My stomach drops.

This one's a goodie.

We were parked on PCH, windows down, car console packed with beach food (fried clams, french fries, lemonade in frosty bottles). The wind that whipped our cheeks was cold and salty, and we laughed and danced in our seats with the radio, shoving our faces full of batter and grease, grinning stupidly while the waves outside crashed and retreated. I was happy, Dan. I'd been a miserable idiot until you came along, and now I was like one of those giggle toys that laugh hysterically when you punch them in the gut.

"More ketchup, please."

"Here." You passed me a couple of packets. "Nat?"

"Hmm?"

"I love you."

I had a fry hanging out of my mouth. "You love me?" I'd waited four long months for those words, and now here they were—I! love! you!—so casual! So breezy! As if you'd been saying them every day, always. "Dan, I—" I tried saying them back and a chunk of potato fell from my lips. You laughed so loud it rocked the car.

"I hate you!" I threw the fry at your face.

"No you don't."

"You're right, I love you."

"Say it again."

"I love you."

"One more time."

"I love you!" I said, and then we crazy made out for an hour.

It was the best, Dan. Better than our first kiss. Better than birthday cake or methamphetamines or the chicken wraps from the Lebanese place by your house. This moment MATTERED. Love meant devotion and commitment and FOREVER. You kissed me and cradled my face with your hands. I felt high. Higher than if I'd been mainlining coffee and candy all morning long. I thought for sure this feeling would last—the elation and excitement—and I couldn't imagine a time when you weren't in my life, loving me; when I wasn't loving you.

Truth is, I still love you and I loathe you for it.

Because somewhere along the way you stopped loving me back.

Nat

She's wrong, I didn't stop loving her. A little piece of me will likely always love Nat, but being enmeshed with someone *that* dynamic, *that* seductive but scary turbulent—it comes with a cost. One I could never sort out a way to pay without going into overdraft.

Last fall, at about the midway point in our relationship, Nat had a collage piece in a group show at Marlborough; her fancy-as-fuck, all-girls school in Hancock Park. Nat's parents were there, Lex too, but I spent most of the night on my own browsing mediocre student art—lumpy sculptures and sloppy sketches—while Nat held court with a gaggle of fawning peers and faculty.

"See anything you like?" It was Lex, saving me. I'd been on my own slurping too-sweet punch for an hour, contemplating escape routes. "I think the Renoir knockoff is for sale."

"But likely out of my price range," I joked.

Lex bit down on a spray-cheese-slathered cracker. "You should've been here for last year's show. Katherine Felps took a dump in the middle of the studio and had the balls to call it art."

I blinked, stunned. "You're shitting me."

"Ha! But no, I'm dead serious." She finished her snack with a shrug. "Sheesh, private school!"

I laughed, despite myself. I liked Alexa. She was brash and a little scary but in a pleasant, disarming way.

"You like Nat's piece?" she asked after a beat.

In fact, I loved it. It was her best yet; an eerie, animalistic self-portrait. "I do, yeah. A lot."

"Nancy Schattner wants to buy it for her private collection."

"Who?"

"Marlborough board member." She ladled some neon punch into a clear plastic cup. "And Schattner's husband says he has a journalist friend who might be interested in doing a profile on Nat for the Arts & Culture section of the L.A. Times."

My body went rigid. "The *Times*?" I looked across the room at Nat. She was radiating something I hadn't seen before tonight: a blinding, incandescent ray of—*what*? Pride? Self-assurance? Suddenly I was seeing her the way others seemed to: as *special. Inventive.* Nat wasn't like everyone else our age. She had *it.* That unnamable quality. That undefinable appeal that could launch her into a galaxy of insane success and fame. She was "a visionary," people were saying. "A unique talent." She was going to go far with or without her parents' money; whether *I* felt threatened or not.

"Wanna go outside and smoke a blunt?" Lex said.

"Huh?" I couldn't look away from Nat. I felt a fast, sweet pang of adoration, of *love*, that was quickly obliterated by a wallop of jealousy. "I don't smoke pot."

"Me neither, *duh.*" She smiled impishly then ran for the exit. "I was just testing you!"

I downed my punch, waved at Nat, and checked my phone. Three texts from Arielle.

She'd been messaging me all weekend long—You're cute; You're trouble; I know you're taken, but—flirtatious nonsense that I hadn't responded to. Not really, anyway.

"Hi, you." Nat was here now, kissing me; pawing my face/shoulders/neck. "Sorry for leaving you alone for so long." She grabbed my phone and—"Who's been keeping you busy while I've been so hideously neglectful?"—checked my screen.

Panicked, I took my cell back and blurted, "No one," but it was already too late. Nat had seen the messages and her eyes were now wild with shiny, It-Girl tears.

"Dan?"

"She's basically stalking me," I insisted, shrugging coolly, though in actuality, I'd been the one to initiate the conversation that night. I'd texted earlier right after meeting Nat's art teacher, Leilani, who had called Nat's portrait "sensational" and "strikingly violent."

"I barely wrote back, see?" I thrust the phone in Nat's face. My side of the chat was all acronyms and evasive emojis. She didn't care though. She kept crying anyway. Quietly, but a few passersby noticed. I pulled her outside onto the patio where it was windy and warm. The Santa Anas were blowing everything sideways and down—palm trees, people, street signs.

"Tonight was so important to me," she murmured.

I felt a blip of guilt followed by a furious wave of justification. Nat had been getting all the attention after all. Hadn't I deserved some too?

"Is something going on with that girl, Dan?"

"She's just a friend."

"But do you like her more than me?"

I didn't. I wished I did. Arielle seemed so uncomplicated. The kind of girl who goes through boys like bags of potato chips. She seemed spacey and noncommittal and, frankly, like fun. I wanted to want her. I wanted to want a girl who wasn't an emotionally unhinged creative genius. But Nat, *Christ*, for better or worse, *she* had my heart. "I don't like her more than you," I said, pulling her close; thinking a hug or a nuzzle might soothe her. If only we could level the playing field; get back to that space where we were both at our best: *Boxed mac and cheese. Wall-to-wall carpeting.*

"Please say you still love me?" Nat said, chin quivering, eyelashes wet and fluttering. And I did of course, so, "I do," I said, but the love I felt—it was tight and constricting like a straightjacket.

AlexaMcKay17: I spy your green, glowing dot . . .

N_Fierro: Sexy Lexy!

AlexaMcKay17: You weren't in calc Friday.

N_Fierro: I cut. Dan and I went to Malibu.

N_Fierro: Lex.

AlexaMcKay17: Nat.

N_Fierro: He loves me.

AlexaMcKay17: He said it??

N_Fierro: Flipping finally, yeah!

AlexaMcLay17: How's it feel???

N_Fierro: Uh, fantastic??

AlexaMcKay17: Nat! Can we celebrate?

N_Fierro: Yes! When?

AlexaMcKay17: Tomorrow after school? Village Pizza?

N_Fierro: Can't! Dan's got the day off so we're checking out some
rando vintage mall in the Valley. What about Thursday after Quigley's
lecture?

AlexaMckay17: I have debate.

N_Fierro: Next week?

AlexaMcKay17: You seriously don't have anything sooner?

N_Fierro: Ah, no??

AlexaMcKay17: I've never had to schedule plans with you WEEKS in
advance before.

N_Fierro: Please don't be mad, Lex. I'm in love!

N_Fierro: Are you mad?

N_Fierro: Okay, you're mad.

AlexaMcKay17: You've stood me up twice this month. AND you missed the food fundraiser last week.

N_Fierro: I apologized for that.

AlexaMcKay17: That was a huge deal, coordinating that event.

N_Fierro: I'm sorry!

AlexaMcKay17: And now you're all booked up??

N_Fierro: Please don't act like I'm a super shitty person.

AlexaMcKay17: Did I say you were?

N_Fierro: You're inferring it.

AlexaMcKay17: I can't possibly think you're THAT shitty if I'm sitting here begging for your love like a dog.

N_Fierro: Lex . . .

AlexaMcKay17: It's pathetic.

N_Fierro: It's not.

AlexaMcKay17: This feels bad, Nat! Like, I feel super desperate and weird and like I'm competing with Dan for your attention. And I LIKE Dan. Which makes this worse.

N_Fierro: Stop! Please don't feel that way. It's not you, it's hormones! I feel like I'm on some sort of ecstasy/speed cocktail 24-7. I can't even remember to do everyday shit like shower.

AlexaMcKay17: You must be a charming date.

N_Fierro: Was that a joke?

AlexaMcKay17: That was a joke, yes.

N_Fierro: Good! Don't be mad. Come with us tomorrow?

AlexaMcKay17: To the rando Valley vintage mall?

N_Fierro: Yeah.

AlexaMcKay17: Uh . . .

N_Fierro: Please?? If you come we can do dinner after. Just you and me.

AlexaMcKay17: Really? Just us?

N_Fierro: I'll send Dan home, hand to heart.

AlexaMckay17: Can we get pizza?

N_Fierro: We can.

AlexaMcKay17: Did I guilt you into this?

N_Fierro: 100%.

Time to get a little X-rated.

I'm writing you from bed, scribbling away under a canopy of white Christmas lights and glow-in-the-dark ceiling stars. I'm in my silkiest pajamas thinking dark, lascivious thoughts. Turned on yet? Remember what happened here, nearly a year ago? Twisted up in my sheets, fumbling awkwardly, bouncing back and forth between pain and exaltation?

"You look incredible."

"Do I?"

I was standing on my front stoop wearing your favorite sundress— spaghetti straps, batik print, thin fabric. I'd twisted my hair into a topknot and stuck a gardenia under the elastic.

"Mariella?" you asked, passing me a bouquet of wilted wildflowers.

"She's off today."

"Nervous?"

"Excited. You?"

"Petrified."

I grabbed you, kissed you, then pulled you quickly inside the house.

Upstairs, I'd really tried to create a mood with dim lights and tea lights and fresh-cut jasmine and new sheets; I'd even shoved all my naked, decapitated Barbies into a sock drawer. The room looked legit. Adult. The sun was setting, the light outside, a neon pink; Kitty Carlisle sat stone-like on my bureau, watching us.

"We have an audience," you said, pointing at the cat.

"A true voyeur," I said.

"I want this to be perfect, Nat."

"It will be."

"And, like, I want you to know how much this means to me."

"It doesn't have to be a big deal, Dan."

"It does though. I want it to be."

I scooped up Kitty Carlisle and dropped her onto the hallway rug. Then I locked the door and looked at you. We were alone.

First, it was your hands around my waist, shaky and timid; next, it was your fingers unraveling my bun. Between kisses you slipped the straps from my shoulders and tugged lightly at the sides of my dress. I yanked off your T-shirt. I bit your earlobe. I laughed while you shimmied gracelessly out of your pale, baggy jeans. Within seconds we were on the bed, limbs entwined, bodies hot and bothered. We'd been here before of course— three months in, and we were masters of the Everything-But. This was different though, this was how lovers did it: they got sweaty and primal;

they writhed, they rocked, they made abysmal noises and sounds—

"Nat?" You'd slipped on the condom, slipped inside me, and, "Am I hurting you?"

It was happening. My thighs were slick; my pulse beat quick. I pushed my face into the pillow in an attempt to smother a cry. "Keep going," I told you, bucking reluctantly; clamping my eyes shut and praying you thought my pleasure was pain.

Sex is weird, isn't it? There's something so mind-fucky and thrilling about pretending to be something you're not. The Naughty Nurse. The Wicked Mistress. I'd been so committed to playing my part—Virgin, Amateur, Naïf—I'd even planned to feign pain and fumble awkwardly. Tricky, yes, but I didn't see a way around it. You were a virgin, Dan. You expected me to be one too.

But see, I hadn't expected it to feel so good. First-time sex always sucks. It sucks the first time you do it, and then it sucks each first-time you do it with someone new. Before you, I'd always hated it. Then again, I'd never loved the person I was doing it with. And lying while loving you—all that shame mixed with fuzzy feelings of affection? adoration?—it was, uh, kind of arousing. Shocking, no? Considering your virgin status?

So here's the gist of it: First time I did the deed I was thirteen. It was with my sixteen-year-old neighbor, a homeschooled kid with ADHD who had a recurring role on a popular teen soap. He was sweet, bizarre; he liked me a lot, and I completely screwed him over. We had sex twice. I never called him back after that.

I didn't do it again until I was fifteen when I dated Jason Paruch. He was a Red-Bull-swilling, loafer-wearing, self-centered, self-serving prick. He treated me like shit and I loved it. One time he fucked someone else and I pretended not to notice so he'd stay with me. I was obsessed with him. He's likely the reason why messed-up shit like guilt turns me on. We only went out for five months, but I stalked him for a year after our breakup. Honestly, I don't think I got over him fully until I met you.

There were two more guys after that: Erik Thormahlen and David Friedman. Both went to Harvard-Westlake. I don't know if they knew each other. I only did it with each of them a few times.

So why lie?

Because I honestly didn't think you'd still want me if you knew the truth. Not only was I not a virgin, but I'd been having sex with fair frequency for FOUR YEARS. And this wasn't loving, sweet, relationship sex; this was fucking. And YOU? God, Dan, you were near perfect. Principled and romantic and idealistic and PURE. And you wanted someone equally noble.

So that's what I gave you. The good girl you'd fantasized about. The one you could deflower, defile, make love to.

But you outgrew that fantasy pretty quick, didn't you, D? The more sex we had and the better it got, the less you seemed to love me. Which makes sense, I guess. I mean, it's pretty hard to respect a girl when she's on all fours doing lewd things to you.

FOR you.

You thought you'd landed some saintly Madonna, didn't you, Novio? But in actuality you'd fallen for a whore. Quelle surprise! Jeez Louise! Who can blame you for losing interest?

Natalie

DAN, 11:34 A.M.

My heart's doing some sort of arrhythmic dance.

My hands are so wet they feel washed.

Sometimes, still, when I'm awake late, when I'm dozing in class, I get flashes: Nat, naked, head hanging over me, blunt tips of her hair brushing my face.

Her body, thin and pale, moving under mine.

Silky sheets against smooth skin.

The smell of jasmine mixed with sweat.

It's all so sharp and vivid. Memories I've replayed thousands of times. Now? They're worthless. Each one a colossal fucking lie.

I've been had.

Completely duped.

I did everything right too—I waited for *the* girl, the one with the open heart and awesome mind and huge aspirations and the talent. I picked the whip-smart one, the funny one, the sexy one with sass and morals. I couldn't have cared less if she'd had sex before, regardless of what kind of sex she'd had. But Nat had to go and lie about it. She had to go and rewrite the narrative, manipulate our story.

"I've never done this," she said to me, lashes fluttering. "I'm so scared, Dan."

"What if it hurts?"

"What if I bleed?"

"What if I disappoint you?"

And the whopper: "You're the only guy I could ever imagine doing this with."

I believed all of it: every word, every gesture, every moan/groan/whimper. Which makes me a chump, sure. But am I a sexist idiot like her letter suggests? Am I having some sort of Freudian meltdown?

No.

Because this isn't about what gets me off, this is about our sham of a relationship. About Natalie's lies.

Would I have preferred to have lost it to the inexperienced, virginal girl that I *thought* I was dating? Yeah, of course. But if she had just had enough integrity to come clean with me up front, I still would've wanted her, past or no past.

Too bad she never gave me the chance to prove it.

I straighten up, scan the quad, and pull my phone from my pocket. Arielle's last text is dated 5/6, two weeks ago. Did you take substantial notes in Gloeckner's lecture? If yes, can I borrow? I hadn't responded, my head too full of breakup bullshit.

Now, though? Now I'm feeling more clear.

I type quickly, scared if I think too much I'll wuss out. Where are you? I ask, hitting send.

Her response is almost instantaneous: Chem lab. You?

I'm skipping government. Meet me by west exit?

Now?

I pause, my fingers hovering over the keyboard. Yes, now.

Zero response. I pack my crap up anyway and head for the other side of campus.

Arielle's sitting on a rock when I arrive.

"Wasn't sure you'd be here," I say.

"You call, I come running."

I look down at the cement, feeling awkward. "You wanna walk and talk?"

"Where to?"

"I dunno, out there somewhere?" I wave a hand at the trees beyond the soccer field.

"Can't we just stay here?"

"We could, but—" I try my most encouraging smile. "You're not up for a stroll?"

"I mean . . ." She looks around distractedly then checks her watch. "Did you have something to say to me or not?"

I stiffen, embarrassed and a little confused. "Not specifically, no." I smile again, hoping to shift the mood but she doesn't smile back. She's stony-faced, waiting for a real reply.

"I don't . . ." I look down at the ground, flustered. "I think maybe we got our signals crossed?"

"Our signals?"

I feel my cheeks flush. Have I played a little too hard to get? Is she pissed that I never responded to that last text? "Is this about Gloeckner's lecture?"

"*What?*"

"I just wanted to see you," I say quickly. "I thought maybe you'd want to see me too."

"Dan." She throws a hand up. "Seriously?"

"You can't be mad," I blurt. "I've had a girlfriend all year and we *just* broke up and I—"

"This isn't about—" She stops then starts again. "I have a boyfriend too, you know."

"I know that."

"And we're not exclusive," she says, which is true, they're not; Whitman's pretty unwavering in his commitment to no-strings sex. "So I haven't been doing anything wrong, talking to you. I'm allowed to, like, hang out with other guys."

"I *know.*"

She looks so small and sad suddenly. Nothing like the brazen flirt who's been sending me coquettish texts all year long. I think about my own situation with Natalie and wonder if Ari's hard-core persistence this year has had less to do with me and more to do with her dissatisfaction with Whitman. "I'm sorry if I did something to upset you."

Her face softens for a second but then quickly bounces back into place. "It's not me you should be saying sorry to." She pauses for a few significant beats. "Call your ex."

Her words send circular shockwaves down and around my

body. "Wait, what?"

"Natalie," she says, eyeing me now, emphasizing each sylla-
ble with icy intonation. "Save your sorries for her, Dan."

JUNE 6, 2015, SATURDAY, 11:45 P.M., TEXT

From: David Friedman

To: Natalie Fierro

What the hell are you, some sort of siren? Temptress? A witch?
I cannot stop thinking about you or your legs or your goddamn
beige Buick. Text back, please. Put me out of my misery.

OCTOBER 29, 2015, THURSDAY, 7:02 A.M., EMAIL

From: Jason Paruch

To: Natalie Fierro

Hey,

Can you please stop driving past my house like a fucking stalker? My
parents think you're batshit. Also, I swear to God, if you don't quit sending
cryptic, threatening texts to Taylor, I'm calling the police.

JP

MARCH 16, 2016, WEDNESDAY, 4:54 P.M., CHAT

Arielle_Schulman: I wanna break up.

TheBenWhitman: No.

Arielle_Schulman: Fuck you.

Arielle_Schulman: Fine.

Hiya!

I'm at our fave spot in Laurel Canyon eating a massive bowl of spaghetti aglio e olio. The candles are flickering; the waiters are bustling; the table crayons, Dan, are calling my name. How's your belly? Rumbling yet? Are you reeling back to that moment when, lit by warm, expensive ambiance, you devoured an entire bowl of tagliolini con tartufo and spent the rest of the night on the pot?

Poor babe. The pukes! The runs! How humiliating that must've been, being THAT wrecked in front of the girl you got busy with! Not that I minded, I liked you that way—vulnerable, a little desperate and needy. I liked being able to provide you with care, comfort, and flat Coke.

"Nat, wake up."

It was three a.m., three weeks into our sex phase, and the sick trolls had just shown up.

"What's going on?" I said, half-asleep still, blinking quickly while wiping the drool from my chin. "You okay?"

"I feel bad, Nat."

Your dad was up north, Jessa was on some science retreat, and my parents were in the desert so we were playing house. "What kind of bad?"

"Like, stomach bad. I think you should go."

"Where?"

"Home."

"What?! No!"

"Nat, please."

"Why?"

"So I can puke in private?"

I got up, switched on the bedside lamp, and looked at you. "Can you keep water down?"

You were flushed and swaying a little. You shook your head.

I grabbed a glass off the nightstand and beelined for the bathroom. "Can you try, at least?"

"Don't go in there!"

It was a frantic plea, but I ignored it, jiggling the doorknob and pushing my way in. Instantly I was hit by the pungent smell of sick. I recoiled and slammed the door shut. "I'm gonna go root around downstairs for supplies. Where do you keep the meds?"

"Dad's bathroom cabinet." You looked mortified. I grabbed one of your sweatshirts off the floor and slid it over my head. Then I set out in search of provisions.

Having never had the chance to explore the house alone before, I had to resist the urge to spend hours in your mother's closet—that walk-in time capsule that your dad kept so pristine. I'd always been really curious about it; I'd seen Jessa rummaging around in there once, trying on rings and pendants, smelling your mom's old clothes. I'd been intrigued, not being able to conjure up similar feelings of sentimentality about my own mother. Was yours really that glamorous? That kindhearted and loving? I still didn't know. I'd asked, of course, but you'd always dodged my questions.

"Was she one of those moms who wore, like, Chanel No. 5 and chandelier earrings?"

"Huh?"

"Like a real movie star mom, you know? Or like a beauty queen?"

"I dunno, Nat. She was very pretty, sure. But she was a nurse."

She was the part of you I could never access; the part you protected so fiercely. She was the Other Woman, Dan. One of several, I now know, but your mom—she was the original.

So I only managed a quick dip in the Closet. I pulled out a dress or two, fingered the silk and the linen, dabbed my wrists with her rose oil and swiped on some lipstick. Then I headed downstairs to put the kettle on.

Fifteen minutes later I returned with a tray full of crap: Pepto, hot tea, ginger ale, stale saltines, a warm washcloth, a bottle of activated charcoal. You were stretched sideways on the bed, breathing raggedly.

"Here," I said, handing you two capsules and the soda.

"What the hell are these?"

"Charcoal. They use it in hospitals for drug overdoses." I'd learned that the hard way after going a little crazy with some Oxycodone one time. "It'll soak up whatever's making you sick."

"You found this in Dad's cabinet?"

"Jessa's. Hippie girls on YouTube use it to whiten their teeth. Come on, swallow."

You sat up, took the pills, then fell backward onto the bed. "When I promised you a romantic night, this isn't exactly what I had in mind."

"I don't care," I said, meaning it, dropping the tray onto your nightstand. "You wanna watch TV?"

"Okay, but you can totally take Jessa's bed. Get some sleep?"

"No. I wanna watch super cheesy infomercials with my boyfriend."

You mustered a smile. "Don't say 'cheese,' please."

"Right, sorry!" I tossed you the remote and grabbed the hot washcloth. "You want this?"

"Please."

I folded it lengthwise and pressed it to your head. "Good?"

"Yeah."

"Too hot?"

"No, perfect." You clicked on the TV. "Nat?"

"Hmm?"

"Thanks for babying me."

It was the perfect thank you—sincere and sad. I wondered if you missed this kind of thing with your mom gone; wondered if your dad ever doted on you, or Jessa; wondered when the last time you truly felt cared for

was—was it when She was still around? I wanted to fill that void, Dan;
to comfort you, to provide you with those feelings of security and safety. I
wanted to love you and baby you and BE your baby and buy you things
and screw you and marry you and be your mistress.

"Are you wearing lipstick?" you asked.

I wanted to be your everything.

And for one brief moment, while watching you take chalky shots of
Pepto-Bismol, I got to be.

X, N

Thinking about that night—picturing Nat pawing my mother's things while I was upstairs, oblivious, shitting my brains out?—makes me sick. No one could ever, *ever,* replace my mom, least of all Natalie, with her self-absorption, her erratic moods, her crazy manipulations and stunts—

"Did she look like you?"

We only talked about her once in earnest, while walking up Hillhurst looking in shop windows.

"I mean, no?" I said, passing Nat the ice cream we'd been sharing. My mother had been dead two years at this point, which may seem like a long time but it still felt pretty fresh. "Jessa's more my mom—the blond hair and the eyes? I'm my dad, I think."

"No way," Nat said, scrunching her nose up. "He's, like, grumpy looking."

"You think my dad's grumpy?"

"*Looking,*" she said with a sigh. "Like, intense, you know? Those eyebrows?" She bit the tip of her spoon. "How'd they meet, anyway?"

"College party."

"So they were practically high school sweethearts, like us."

"I mean, give or take four years."

She smiled wistfully. "He seems to really miss her."

"He does, a lot."

"That's sad though, right?" She dipped her spoon into the chocolate and swirled it around distractedly. "But also, like, kind of beautiful? That he's still so torn up? Do you think it's because their love was really that exceptional? Or is his devotion, like, a death thing?"

I stiffened. "Like a death thing?"

"Right. Like how when people die they're suddenly sainted. Like Carrie Dressman who killed herself my freshman year. No one liked her and then she died, and everyone wept for weeks."

"What does that have to do with my mother?"

"Huh?" Nat snapped to. "Oh, nothing. Well, not nothing I guess. I was just wondering if death makes you better. Like, it seems to kinda wipe the slate clean, you know?"

"No."

"*Yes*, come on, you do! It's interesting, right? How it skews people's perspectives?" She laughed and grabbed me. "God, I should kill *my*self. I'd be way more popular with the Marlborough crowd."

I wanted to punch something—a wall, a tree, a face. "You think my mother couldn't have possibly been that great?" I pulled away. "That her relationship with my dad wasn't special? That my memories are, like, delusions?"

Her eyes got big. "That's not what I said." She tried touching my face but I flinched. "I was speaking hypothetically."

"You didn't even know my mother."

"I know that."

"You've never lost anyone."

"I know. *Hey.*" She reached for me. "I wasn't trying to hurt you or, like, shit all over your mom. I'm sure she was great."

"That's an understatement."

"Okay, sorry."

I could barely hear her, my head so clouded with rage still. "And what the hell with the suicide joke?"

She hesitated a second. "Who said I was joking?"

Suddenly, as if shocked by some shoddy electrical socket, I wanted out. "I'm taking you home," I said, grabbing her elbow roughly, hanging a right onto Finley.

"Dan, come on!" She tripped trying to keep up. "I'm not going to *do* anything about it, obviously. It's just a thought that comforts me when I feel really bad or anxious."

"Dying isn't romantic."

"I didn't say it was." She got loose and jogged a few feet ahead of me; flipping around so we were face to face. "I just think—it's inevitable, right? We're all gonna die one day, so what's so wrong with wanting to control the how and the when of it?"

"So you wanna kill yourself?"

She laughed. "Not currently, no."

"But you've thought about it."

"I have, yeah." She said this casually, as if she'd just said instead, *I'll take another wine spritzer with lime.* "But not, like, seriously or anything."

We'd reached the car and I was fumbling now, trying to find my keys.

"Are you hearing me?" she asked, slipping a hand around my waist and under my shirt; shocking my skin with cold fingers. "Things are good right now. *We're* good. You make me happy, Dan."

"I can't be your savior."

"But you are, you're my hero."

"But I don't want to be."

She pulled away—"Jesus Christ, way to wreck a moment"— walked to the passenger side, then tugged futilely, repeatedly, on the door handle. "Can you let me in?"

I regretted the savior thing instantly. "Look—"

"Can you let me in?" she said again.

"Yeah," I whispered feebly. I turned the key and the lock popped.

From: Ruth Schwarzbein

To: Dan Jacobson; Jessa Jacobson

Guys, see attached. It's your mom and me in our early twenties in the old complex in North Beach. Photo was taken right after a party we threw in celebration of Bastille Day—Joyeux Quatorze Juillet! Ridiculous. I was a complete Francophile then.

Notice the smoke wafting from your mother's hand—that's a joint, not a cigarette! Such rebellion. Don't do drugs, kids!

Love,

Auntie Ruthie

From: Paul Jacobson

To: Dan Jacobson

I'm letting Jessa choose the restaurant this year, you okay with that? She wants Vietnamese, Bánh mì specifically, she seems to think it's something Mom would've been into.

Can I trust you with the cake? Bring two packs of birthday candles, she would've been forty-eight this year.

—Dad

From: Jessa Jacobson

To: Dan Jacobson

That jacket you wore out today is hideous. Mom would've hated it. Where'd you get that thing? Natalie? Why do all rich girls love ugly clothes?

10

Hey,

So I'm in Joshua Tree at my parents' cabin, where you and I spent our one and only weekend away together. Remember the fun we had here? Guzzling wine by the fire pit? Screwing against cold adobe walls? Watching tumbleweeds somersault across dusty, barren landscapes? It was the best, Dan—the freezing nights and blazing days, the 24-7 lovefest. It was the best until—you guessed it—it was the absolute worst.

"Aya-what?"

"Ayahuasca," I said, stretching the word this time. We were camped out on the scratchy turquoise rug, late-day sun hitting us sideways while we ate from a crate of clementines. "My mother hosts these druggie ceremonies where she and her friends drink ayahuasca in the teepee out back and then hallucinate for hours while this shaman leads them all to spiritual enlightenment."

107

"You're messing with me."

"Hand to God I'm not."

You ate an orange slice then leaned in for a citrus-scented kiss. "Are we going out later? Pappy and Harriet's, maybe?"

"Yes, please!" I'd been waiting years to take a date to my favorite desert saloon. "I brought the perfect dress for the occasion. Wanna see?"

Your cell dinged. I grabbed the phone and scanned the text preview. "It's Ruby," I said, deflating. "'SOS.'"

"Her mom's having thyroid surgery and she's freaking out," you said, dialing back already. "Put the dress on, okay?" You headed outside to the deck. "I'll only be one sec."

You took twelve minutes, I counted. I watched you through the sliding glass doors; watched you be the good guy that you are; watched your face pucker and contort in familiar ways. You were just being you, of course—inquisitive, caring, attentive—only now you were being you with HER.

"She okay?" I asked afterward, even though I couldn't have cared less if she was okay. I was standing barefoot on the scratchy rug in my spaghetti strap dress, dying for you to see me.

"You look phenomenal," you said regretfully, sans smile. Your lips were hard and horizontal and—"Nat."

I shook my head and shook my head but—

"Nat, I'm so sorry. Her mom had a bad reaction to the anesthesia and now she's on machines and shit and Ruby's losing her mind and—"

"Is she dying?"

"No! No, she's okay, but she's all screwed up on drugs and babbling *and—"*

"Then you're not leaving."

"I have to."

"No you don't. We can go back early tomorrow, but—" I grabbed the car keys off the dining room table and clutched them tightly. "Pappy & Harriet's, remember?"

"She's hysterical."

"So what?"

"So WHAT?" Your face went all flat like a deflated balloon.

"Yeah, she's gonna live, right? So what's the rush?"

Now you were pissed, your tiny eyes shrinking and shining. "What if it were your mom, huh?"

"If it were my mom, that'd be different," I said. "But it's not my mom, Dan, it's Ruby's, and she's not your girlfriend."

"I've known her a hell of a lot longer than I've known you. That's gotta count for something."

Well you might as well have slapped me.

"Fuck off," I said, throwing the keys on the floor then beelining for the bedroom. "Go be her knight in shining armor then." I scratched at my straps and let the dress fall to my feet.

"You're being a baby."

"I am a baby, asshole!" I was naked now, quivering in my underwear, rageful and near tears. "Fucking GO already."

"Natalie."

"Go!"

"There's one car," you said, eyebrows bouncing. "What're you gonna do? Stay here until you run out of oranges?"

Something inside me cracked. I dropped to the floor, sobbing. "I hate her so much."

You crouched down and rubbed my bare back. "She was there for me, Nat." I could barely see you through the fog of my tears. "When my mom was sick," you said, softening, "she was there."

Well screw me.

Ruby Lefèvre may be a bland girl made of bland things—vanilla soft serve and saltine crackers and plain spaghetti—but shit, Dan, she sure has your heart. "Fine," I said, feeling horrible but accepting defeat. "Ruby wins again." I wiped my wet cheeks, grabbed a T-shirt off the ground, and stood up.

"It's not a competition, Nat."

I wasn't so sure about that. And I don't think you were either.

Ms. Lefèvre lived, of course—they switched her anesthetic and then successfully yanked out her thyroid. Ruby, you told me, cried nonstop until the surgery was over. Sobbing on your shoulder, no doubt. Clinging to you like Saran Wrap. Riding that wavy line between friend-in-need and oh-just-fuck-me-already.

I have never, EVER trusted that girl, Dan.

You, I trusted.

Huge mistake.

Nat

Well shit, she knows.

I'm surprised it took her this long to say it. That's either some insane herculean restraint, or she's got this number choreographed and timed to the minute. Wonder what comes next. Public torture? My crucifixion?

To be clear, nothing happened with Ruby that weekend. Nat and I drove back to LA in a silent cloud of misery, and then I went straight to the hospital.

"I wrecked your big trip," Ruby said, weaving through the waiting area; looking teary and red-nosed in a ratty T-shirt and baggie jeans. "Is she pissed?"

"Livid," I said, closing the distance between us; smiling then pulling her into a too-tight embrace. "How's your mom?"

"She couldn't stop puking this morning. Now they've got her on saline and anti-nausea meds. Seems to be helping."

"What about you, have you eaten?"

"I've been watching her barf all day."

"Right. Coffee maybe? Tea?" I rubbed her icy hands. "You're freezing."

"Think I need something a little stronger than tea."

"Whiskey shooter?"

"Morphine drip."

"Well, Lefèvre," I slipped an arm around her shoulders and walked her toward the elevators, "you've come to the right place."

"I miss your mom," Ruby said not too long after that. We were sitting on a manicured plot of grass in the hospital courtyard, clutching hot, disposable cups. "She made the best snacks."

"Peanut butter crackers."

"Chocolate chip oatmeal cookies."

"Tahini dip."

"Fried artichokes."

"I miss her too," I said, digging a hand into the dirt; uprooting a lone weed with my middle finger. "But yours is gonna be fine."

"I know," she said, smiling for several seconds before losing her shit completely; folding forward, heaving deeply into shaky hands.

"Ruby, it's okay."

"How does somebody who lives on pearled freaking barley get thyroid cancer?"

"I don't think we have the kind of control that we think we do."

"That's terrifying."

"Or liberating."

"I'm sorry," she said, wincing a little, her voice tinged with guilt. "I didn't mean to suggest that your mom—that she did something wrong and that that's why she got sick."

"I knew what you meant." I grabbed her hand and squeezed reassuringly.

"I don't understand how you do it," she said, smiling sadly, squeezing back. "This feeling, Dan, it's like suffocating. I feel like"—another tear blast—"like if she dies, I'll die."

"She's not gonna die," I said, touching her chin then tilting her face up. "Listen to me. *She's not dying.* Something scary happened, but it's being fixed."

I said this, but could I really be certain? After all, promises had been made to me when my mom was sick too.

"You're sure?" she asked, blinking back tears, lashes batting like insect wings.

"I mean, can I guarantee you that your mom won't be out running errands next month and get hit by a bus? No. But do I think she'll survive a little thyroid cancer? Ruby, yes."

She fell forward in relief, her head whapping my chest. "You and your mom—you were all I could think about all morning long."

I stroked her hair, my fingers catching in her tangled curls.

"You must miss her so much."

"I do."

I missed school-supply shopping and long drives and trips to the orthodontist and Sunday bakeoffs and mornings with bagels and lox and shitty coffee, and I missed—

"I miss just, like, smelling her, you know?"

"Man, *yes*, she smelled great, didn't she? Like flowers but fresh ones." Ruby's fingers made whisper-light figure eights on my forearm.

"Hey!"

It's Ruby in real-time looking flushed and frazzled. *Ruby*, who I've been avoiding now for nearly six weeks.

"I texted earlier," she says, and I'm instantly babbling defensive nonsense like—

"Today's been crazy, and I'm sorry I didn't get back to you but—"

"No, Dan, *look*." She slams a starched, ragged piece of canvas against my locker, the surface covered with colorful scraps of construction paper—tiny faces all arranged to make one larger face. One that looks exactly like Ruby. "Is that . . . ?"

"A Fierro original?" She drops the collage into my lap. "I'm gonna go out on a limb and say yes."

The eyes have been blacked out with jagged strips of inky silk. The mouth is open and screaming; a dark cave brightened only by a snake tongue made up of hundreds of miniscule red, broken hearts. It's long and cruel-looking and forks at the tip; its ends slithering up the sides of the portrait like bitter, vindictive serpents.

"Wow."

"I mean, what the hell *is* this?" she says. "A threat?"

It's for sure a threat. "I mean, maybe?"

"I'm guessing she knows, then?"

"I think so, yeah."

She drops her backpack and slumps down next to me. "Are you guys still in contact?"

I consider telling her about the letters but stop myself. No use throwing gasoline on a wildfire. "Not exactly."

"Not exactly?"

"Can we not talk about this right now?" Nat, Ruby, Ari—it's all just too much. "I have Ryan's graduation at five today, and I need to stay focused."

"Should I set something up with your assistant for later this week, Werner Herzog?"

"I just need a break."

"From what? From *me*?"

"I just—" What's my excuse? I've been an avoidant, cowardly asshole for weeks. "I've just been overwhelmed with the Nat situation and with school and with—"

"Right, I know, your *film*. Jesus Christ, you're insufferable." She stands quickly, stepping on the collage. "Sorry to bother you with my bullshit feelings of loss and abandonment. Tell your crazy ex to stop sending me creepy threats."

I feel the hot flush of shame and shoot up. "Ruby, wait." She isn't waiting; she's tearing down the hallway, her book bag bouncing off her round hip. "Ruby!" I chase after her, catching up.

"What?" she says, whipping around, irate. *"Now* you wanna talk?"

"Yes, I'm sorry."

"For which part?"

"For avoiding you after we . . ." I can't say it. I'm too chickenshit.

"After we *what,* Dan?"

"Ruby, please, every time I see you I see *her* in my head and I—"

"Stop talking about Natalie!" she screams, her voice thick and breaking. "My God, you're not even *with* her anymore and you're still obsessing!"

"I'm sorry," I say again, and this time it's with real remorse.

"She's still in your head, like, manipulating you."

"That's not it." That's exactly it though, isn't it?

"I don't want to be your friend anymore," Ruby says, bottom lip trembling.

"Rubes." My heart hurts. A hulking kid with a massive gym bag rams right into her and she barely flinches. I feel like scum. Like coffee dregs. I'm tired and pissed at myself and pissed that I've lost everyone that matters: my mom, Nat, now Ruby. "I miss you," I whisper, and I feel guilty saying it, like somehow admitting that I need Ruby makes me this bad, shitty guy.

"So have me," she says, and she's wide open—eyes big with big tears and big need. I swear I can see inside her soul and it's breathtaking but fucking frightening, and I'm suffocating under the pressure of all her intensity and heartache. I *cannot* handle this version of Ruby. The crying Ruby, the desperate Ruby, the Ruby that pines and pleads and makes me feel like an indecisive prick. I don't like that she can tell me with one pained glance that I'm spineless and cowardly and selfish and horny and that I'm the kind of guy who nearly screws a girl he loves a lot but who he has no intention of dating. She reminds me that I'm *that* guy. The guy I hate. The guy I never set out to be.

"I want to be with you," she blurts, eyes flitting sideways and up.

I never should've started this. "I can't be your boyfriend, Ruby."

"And why not?"

"Because that's not who we are, you and me. We're not like that." I smile even though I feel fucking awful. "We're friends."

Ruby's jaw tenses. She smooths her curls with one hand and takes a step back. "I don't get naked with my friends, Dan."

"Right."

"I didn't think you did either."

She's not crying anymore. She's rigid and stoic, and suddenly something's shifted. The air around us feels icy and dry. The overhead fluorescents are buzzing, casting an extra-blue hue on Ruby's face.

"I wrecked us, didn't I?" I say quietly.

Ruby just stands there for a minute, blinking. "You obliterated us," she says back before turning and walking away.

JANUARY 15, 2013, TUESDAY, 3:41 P.M., TEXT

From: Mom

To: Dan

Baby boy, be out front at 4:00 sharp, okay? Is Ruby with you? I've got Gram's wedding ring in the glove compartment waiting to go for whenever you've worked up the courage to propose. ;)

JANUARY 10, 2017, TUESDAY, 11:18 P.M., CHAT

Audra_Rey: Pretty sure something significant just happened with my future husband.

M_Haney: He said ILY?

Audra_Rey: Close. I was at Jessa's earlier helping her shoot a Q&A for her channel, and when I went upstairs to use the bathroom he brushed past me and totally eye-fucked me and winked and went, "Cute dress, Rey."

M_Haney: Shut up.

Audra_Rey: I know!

M_Haney: WHAT WERE YOU WEARING, REY?

Audra_Rey: A CUTE FUCKING DRESS, HANEY!

M_Haney: Is he still with Natalie?

Audra_Rey: According to Jessa, yes, but she says he's miserable. What's that shit called when you derive pleasure from other people's pain?

M_Haney: Schadenfreude.

Audra_Rey: I think I have that. Am I a terrible person, hoping they break up?

M_Haney: Maybe?

M_Haney: God I hope they implode.

Audra_Rey: Me too. Schadenfreude. That's a good word.

M_Haney: I know. Everything sounds better in German.

11

Hola, Novio!

I'm in the hills behind the Hollywood sign, reliving the hike that wrecked all hikes for me: Griffith Park, way west of Ferndale—steep trails, panoramic views, succulents, horse shit, wildflowers, dogs off leashes—just being here makes me want to bash my head against a brick. I used to love this place, Dan. Like really, truly love it. Now it makes me nauseated and sad—two hallmarks of devastating heartbreak, I guess.

"Hey."

It'd been nearly a week since Joshua Tree, and you and I had barely spoken save for a few nonsense texts about Ms. Lefèvre and her surgery. So when we finally met up at the trailhead I was feeling completely unhinged—shaky and weepy and—

"Hi," *I said back, ignoring your sour expression, trying to hide my nerves with a bright, fake grin.* "Which way?" *I waved at the fork in the path.*

"To the stables or the sign?"

"This way," you said, leading me left toward Sunset Ranch.

"Everything cool?" I asked, because things felt irrefutably UNcool. You were two steps ahead of me at all times, pummeling the ground with your black, cleated sneakers.

"I've just spent all week trying to get a bunch of parents to sign consents so I can shoot Ryan's commencement."

"Oh." I was both relieved and disappointed that your mood had nothing to do with me. "Any holdouts?"

"Three. And if they don't sign, I'm screwed. Like, seriously up shit's creek. Without graduation, the movie has no arc."

"That's not true."

You made a face then looked down. "What's all over your shirt?"

"Oh." Embarrassed, I brushed some crap off my tank. "Cornmeal. I was helping Mari make tortillas for my mother's thing tonight."

"Thing?"

"Yeah, she's got an event. Are you breaking up with me?"

Your eyes went all round and wide. "No?"

"No?" I mimicked. Your no swung upward—a question, not a statement.

"Because, like, last week was weird, right? And then this week was weird too?"

"I mean, weird's kind of an understatement."

My stomach flipped.

"It was bad, Nat. Ms. Lefèvre was legitimately sick and you wouldn't let me leave."

"I know, but—" It was shitty, true, but feeling the urge to justify my tantrum, I said, "You can live without a thyroid."

"Natalie."

"I'm sorry!"

"We fight nonstop."

We did, we absolutely did, but, "Doesn't everyone?"

"Fight like that? No. And I think—" You stuttered a bit before delivering the kicker, "I think maybe we need to spend some time apart."

My heart seized. My stomach hit the ground. "You just swore we weren't breaking up."

"We're not."

"I can do better," I said quickly, frantic to fix the mess. "I'll stop being jealous and crazy, and I'll trust you more and—"

"It's not a big deal," you insisted. "I'm not talking about TONS of time. I just think we need to miss each other a little." You weren't looking at me. You were watching the skyline—smoggy and dotted with tall buildings and jagged mountaintops. "Get some perspective, you know?"

I was desperate not to cry. To keep everything in check. To show you that I could be reasonable and levelheaded even though I didn't feel reasonable or levelheaded at all. "But I miss you all the time," I said. "I miss you right now, and we're only inches apart."

"Nat."

I couldn't do it; I didn't have the strength of will not to cry.

"Nat, it's okay." You were petting me while I wept into your ratty flannel. "We're not breaking up."

"Then why does it feel like we are?"

"Look at me."

I tried. You were laughing a little but eyeing me soberly.

"We just need to set some boundaries."

"That sounds horrible. Have you been reading a ton of self-help lately?"

"I'm trying to make things better for us."

"So we're not breaking up?"

"We're not breaking up," you said, taking my face and kissing it gently.

"We're just doing a little experiment."

"What, like, research and development?"

"Exactly."

I kissed you back and hugged you hard. I had trouble letting go.

Three days later, after not texting or talking much, I tried calling you. It was a Friday, and usually you were home Fridays but not that night—your phone was switched off. Normally I would've panicked straightaway, but I reminded myself—we were testing out a new normal, trying to create boundaries, trying to fight less and trust more. So I went downstairs and made a toaster waffle before trying you again. Straight to voice mail. I played two rounds of Crazy Eights with Mariella then tried again. Voice mail. I showered. Voice mail. I texted Lex. Voice mail. I drank half a pint of vanilla vodka then fell asleep in my parents' empty whirlpool tub. Élégant, non?

Turns out, you were with Ruby again. Which of course you lied about.

Asshole.

N

DAN, 1:01 P.M.

I was with Ruby that night, but I wasn't *with* Ruby. We were at the silent movie theater on Fairfax for a rerelease of *Seven Up!*, the first in a series of English docs about kids in the sixties. My phone was switched off. It wasn't until afterward—after the movie, after the Lebanese food, after the ice cream and the night hike and the drive home—that I realized I'd been disconnected from Planet Earth. I switched on my cell and saw all *eleven* of Nat's messages. Four hours' worth of voice mails that started off relatively sane and devolved into psychotic, drunk babble:

"*Hey, it's me. Miss you.*"

"*Hi again, call me back.*"

"*Just freaking out a little. Call when you can?*"

"*So wait, what, your phone died?*"

"*Please explain to me how you can go three days
     without calling your girlfriend? No text,
     no email, no fucking FaceTime? Your space
     experiment is bullshit.*"

"*Lemme guess: Arielle Schulman?*"

"*Maybe your phone's drowning in a pool of Ms.
     Lefèvre's thyroid replacement pills?*"

"*If you're fucking fucking someone, I swear to
     God I'll kill myself.*"

"*I'm sorry.*"

"*Sorry again. I'm just freaked out about that*

hike. Please call me? Please?"

"Fuck. You."

I called back immediately, but she didn't pick up. I tried again the next morning, but my call went straight to voice mail. By midday I was worried—her hysteria over the relationship plus her Ruby paranoia plus her Ari paranoia plus her love of drama—what if she'd done something stupid?

Jessa had the car that afternoon so I took the bus to Nat's place.

"You're alive," I said, standing breathless and sweaty at her doorstep, having just jogged the half mile uphill to her house from the bus stop. "I've been calling you all day."

She was in pajamas still (boxers, see-through tank, no bra) leaning against the doorframe, picking her fingernails. "Yeah, I called *you* all night."

"I know, I got your messages." I was annoyed now that I could see that she was perfectly fine. "All *eleven* of them."

Nat winced and walked inside, leaving the door wide open.

"Hey!" I said, following her up the steps, chasing her bare feet as they slapped the wood floorboards all the way to her room. "Are you gonna say something?" I asked, bumping the bedroom door shut with my back.

She locked eyes with me. "Just tell me you were shooting last night."

I hadn't been. So I didn't.

"What then? Was it that girl?" Her brows and shoulders moved upward in short, sharp jerks. *"Arielle?"*

"No," I said, anger coming to a roiling boil in my gut. Did I really owe her an explanation? A breakdown of yesterday's schedule? I'd asked for a little time and distance, and she'd agreed. So why were we having this talk? *"Eleven* messages."

Nat flushed red and then shifted from leg to leg. "And?"

"And is that what you call giving me space?"

I saw a quick flash of shame cross her face before her mouth hardened into something more stiff. "You're seriously not gonna tell me where you were last night?"

"We had a deal."

"A *deal*?" She said it slowly as if trying to understand the word. "Is that what we are now, some sort of business arrangement? Do I only get to have feelings for you on Wednesdays and alternate weekends?"

"You're twisting my words."

"What about screwing, Dan? Do we have to set up some sort of system for fucking? I only get laid if I let you screw someone else first?"

I was so filled with rage I could've kick-boxed through a plate-glass window. "Stop it."

"Why didn't you just dump me on that hike last week, huh? You wanted to, right?"

I *had* wanted to but I hadn't been able to pull the trigger.

Why?

"You act like I'm the only one behaving badly in this relationship, but you've been checked out from the very beginning," she said. "Where *were* you when my mom had her Hammer event, huh? Or when I got my wisdom teeth out last spring? Or how about this summer when Lex worked so hard to get us those Bowl tickets and you completely bailed last minute? Where were you *then*?"

"You know where I was," I said, my voice an angry, low grumble. "I was filming."

"But when are you *not* filming, Dan?" She blew back her bangs in frustration. "I'm equally committed to my work, and yet somehow, *magically*, I've managed to make the time and space for our relationship. In fact, forget *me*, what about your family? Or school even? Jessa says you're flunking calc."

"She's being hyperbolic; I'm not flunking calc, *Natalie*." I was livid. "Do you know how hard I have to work just to feel adequate around you and your goddamn mother? Do you know what it's like, dating a girl with a platinum charge card who's never had to work a day in her life?"

She laughed. "Jesus Christ, Dan, you're not a pauper! Your dad's a goddamn tax attorney!"

"Fuck you!"

"No, fuck *you*! What is up with the permanent chip on your shoulder, huh? God, your sense of entitlement is *astounding*."

"You *do* realize that if I don't finish my movie I may not get into school? I certainly won't qualify for any scholarship money or grants."

"You have a 3.9 GPA, shithead. You'll get in somewhere."

"And then how will I pay for it? You've fucked off for four years, and you'll probably *still* get into some top-tier art school because your mom's a star and your dad's loaded."

She slapped me.

And I let her because I deserved it.

"I work my ass off in that studio."

"Yeah, you do," I said back, panting, my left cheek throbbing with heat. "And I have to work *twice* as hard because I'm not half as good. You have *everything*, Natalie. Status and money and the fucking talent to back it up."

Her face fell. She took a step toward me then stopped. "Is that a joke?"

"My raging jealousy?" I rubbed my sore cheek and looked down, horrified by the bomb I'd just dropped. "Nope, not a joke. You're just better than me and I hate you for it."

"You *hate* me?"

I didn't. "I don't, no, I just . . ."

"Dan . . ." Her eyes were wide and blazing with pity. "I'm not better than you."

She reached for me and reflexively I backed up. "Please don't."

"Don't *what*?" she said, ignoring me, caressing the side of my head with cold fingers. "I'm sorry I slapped you."

Something inside me broke and I suddenly wanted to bawl. "I can't keep doing this."

She didn't say anything for a second or two. Then her hands slid from my head to my neck. "Dan." I couldn't even look at her. I kept my chin down, but she nudged it upward and said, "Hey. I'm still your girl, right?"

Was she? Did I even want her to be? We locked eyes finally. There she was, my Nat—she looked anxious and vulnerable and near tears. I did a quick scan of her body: the small scar on her chest from where she'd broken her collarbone as a kid; the wave of dark, shiny hair that hid half her face; her skinny legs; her perfect breasts; the tiny constellation of zits on her pale chin. This was how I liked her—a little desperate with a tinge of fragility. I felt a surge of something familiar—lust? love?— and did the only thing I could think to do: I backed away.

But she quickly closed the space between us.

"Dan . . ." was what she said when our foreheads touched, her hip bones poking me like small, dull daggers. "Just tell me where you were last night. Please?"

"I already told you," I said, even though I hadn't told her anything yet. "I was with the Espinosas, shooting. My phone died."

∝

"So you're back together then?" Ruby was standing in my kitchen licking chocolate batter off a spatula.

"I mean, I guess?" I filled a glass with water from the mounted spigot and handed it to Jessa. "Though we were never really broken up."

"They were working out the kinks in their relationship," Jessa offered, sipping the water with her pinkie extended, sounding laughably diplomatic.

"What the hell do *you* know about relationships?" I asked.

"I think she's *in* one," Ruby said, inspecting a spot on Jessa's neck. "I swear to God this is a hickey."

"It's a birthmark!" she screamed, laughing and swatting at Ruby wildly.

"What time does the movie start?" Ruby asked me, arching backward, smiling placidly while Jessa continued to swing.

"I told you I couldn't go, remember?" I was halfway out the door already, frantically searching for my keys. "I'm having dinner with the Fierros."

"You didn't tell me that."

"I did."

"No, Dan, you didn't." She was sober suddenly. "Why do you think I'm here right now?"

"I thought you were helping Jess with her brownie video."

"It's a *lifestyle vlog.*"

"I'm here," Ruby said, "because you and I have plans."

We'd *had* plans, but I'd cancelled them. Hadn't I? "Rubes, I'm sorry, but Nat and I had this whole big talk yesterday about me being more present and I just feel like I *owe* her this, you know?"

She was staring at me, fuming. I stared back. "Don't look at me like that."

"She's manipulating you."

"No," I said, feeling a sudden surge of anger and defensiveness. "We're working things out. Sometimes when you love someone you make sacrifices."

Ruby looked horrified. "Am *I* your sacrifice?"

"I didn't mean *you*."

"No, it's fine," she said, shrugging. "It's totally fine. You *should* ditch me to spend time with her. Even though you and I have known each other since we were thirteen and I've been stupidly loyal while she's been toxic and crazy."

"Oh boy," Jessa said, pushing the brownies aside and then swiftly leaving the room.

"She's my girlfriend, Ruby."

"So? Does that mean I'm not allowed to say something when you blow me off to be with her?"

"You can say whatever you want."

"Great."

"Awesome."

She was staring at me still, jaw clenched, eyebrows raised. I was over it. So sick of bending over backward trying to please, placate, *validate* every single person in my life. I couldn't make Natalie happy without pissing off Ruby. I couldn't make Ruby happy without alienating Nat. I was screwed either way. "What do you *want* from me, Ruby?"

"Nothing," she said, deflating finally, grabbing her bag off the counter then heading for the door.

JANUARY 26, 2017, THURSDAY, 4:52 P.M., EMAIL

From: Joshua G. Velick

To: Jessa Jacobson

Can I please take you on a real date? I don't think the other night counts.

JANUARY 26, 2017, THURSDAY, 9:15 P.M., EMAIL

From: Jessa Jacobson

To: Joshua G. Velick

Okay, here's the thing.

My brother has two girlfriends but thinks he has one. He has the girl he's been stringing along for four years and then the girl he's been officially dating for thirteen months. They hate each other. Both are smart, reasonable girls who get stupid and crazy when they're around him. I'm 85% certain this is his fault. He's a flirt. And he's selfish. Which is fine, and I don't think he's actually screwing multiple people at once, but he can be oblivious and insensitive. And before you start thinking that I hate him, let me just clarify: I LOVE him. He's funny and fun and super supportive, and he bought me a used DSLR for my birthday. Because of him my videos look legit. He's the best. But I would never, EVER want to date him. Watching him throw all that awesome, charming, dramatic bullshit at TWO girls makes me want to barf. It makes me not trust men. Maybe you're nothing like him. Maybe you're a one-woman kind of guy. Maybe you only have eyes for me. Maybe you think I'm an angry man-hater. I'm not. I love dudes. But I'm a delicate flower and most of you scare the living shit out of me.

So I don't know. About the date, I mean.

JANUARY 26, 2017, THURSDAY, 9:22 P.M., EMAIL
From: Joshua G. Velick
To: Jessa Jacobson
Please. I'm nothing like your brother.

12

On our third date I took Nat to a screening of *Sage Rock,* this tiny doc about a commune run by cowboy/rock star/utopian visionary Keith Kelly. Kelly had built an "intentional community" out of an old summer camp in central California, and he had legions of fans and supporters, most of which were rich, influential, famous types. He was a huge deal on the internet, and *Vanity Fair* had profiled him twice. His twenty-year-old daughter, California Kelly, had published a moderately successful tell-all book titled *Growing Up Guru.* The guy was a living legend and I was obsessed with him. Obsessed and pissed that someone—someone older than me with more credentials/money/experience—had gotten to make a film about him first.

"So I've been begging my dad for the last year and a half to let me take a trip up north to see the place," I told Nat as we sat side by side waiting for the movie to start. "It's, like, incredible supposedly: avocado groves, cabins covered in ivy; everything's sustainable and pastured and—"

"I've actually seen it—"

"Pictures don't do this place justice. Have you read the press?"

"No, but—"

"You really should. You'll get a much better sense for Kelly's personality. He's really dynamic and persuasive but not, like, creepy, you know?"

"What, like other cult leaders?"

"It's not a cult," I said. "It's a group of smart, progressive people with a common interest who are exploring an alternative way of life. You should really read up on it, these aren't religious extremists."

Nat smiled placidly and ate a handful of popcorn. "You're really into the guy, huh?"

"Obsessed."

"So you're a socialist?" she said, poking fun. "Into Buddha? Yoga? Self-actualization?"

"I'm into the people who are into it," I said, shaking half a box of Junior Mints into the popcorn.

Later, back at Nat's, we ate chocolate bars and talked about Scientology and *Sage Rock*. I went on and on about how much I'd

hated the film—"It had no vision or, like, unifying theme!"—
and Nat nodded and kissed me and said, "The problem with
that movie is that you didn't make it."

Around eleven, Nat's mom came home looking exhausted
and messy but somehow still glamorous—paint-splattered
denim plus fat diamond ring. "My God," she said, switching on
a light and plopping down on the sofa beside us. "What the hell
are you two doing in the dark? Channeling ghosts?"

"Demons," Nat said, sitting up. "Dan, this is Mae; Mae, this
is Dan."

I shook her small, bedazzled hand. "Really nice to meet
you."

"Yeah," she said, inspecting me. "Nat's crazy about you."

"Can Dan spend the night?"

"What is this, your second date?" Mae grabbed the last piece
of chocolate, inhaling it. "What'd you two end up doing earlier, anyway?"

"Movie," I said, leaning into the couch cushions as Nat stood
up. "We saw *Sage Rock*."

"You saw it?" Mae said to Nat, who was now zigzagging
toward the kitchen. "Shelly Epstein said it was atrocious. I
should ask Dad if he's talked to Keith lately. He must be mortified."

My stomach dropped. *TALKED TO KEITH*. "Talked to
Keith?"

Nat was hiding behind the fridge door.

"Fluff, was it any good?"

"No," she said sheepishly, poking her head out. "It was terrible. It made him seem like a total new age zealot." She looked at me, wincing a little. "I tried to tell you we knew him."

I reeled back in time to our preshow conversation: *I've actually seen it*, she'd said about Sage Rock. *I'VE ACTUALLY SEEN IT.* The words bounced around in my brain like shiny pinballs. She'd been trying to tell me all night and I'd talked over her, eager to impress, wanting to show her that I *knew* things. That I knew about indie docs and hippie communes and sustainability and avocado groves. I hadn't even been interested in *her* side of things, hadn't been looking for a legit exchange, didn't want to hear that she'd googled "*Sage Rock*" and had seen pretty pictures of Kelly devotees meditating. I wanted to tell her that I'd researched the hell out of the place; that if I were older and better connected I'd have made this movie years ago. I'd needed her to know that I was smart, that I liked smart things, that she was dating a fascinating guy. Instead I'd shown her I was a patronizing dick. "I'm sorry," I said. "You must think I'm huge jerk."

"Are you kidding?" she said, shuffling back from the kitchen and curling up beside me on the couch. "I've seen the Dayview footage. You would've done an amazing job with Keith and his cohorts."

She could have annihilated me right then. She could've called me a condescending prick. She could've shamed me, laughed in my face, stomped on me for being an insecure showoff. Instead, she showed her support. Her belief in me. She picked me up and dusted me off and made me feel like a goddamn prince.

"Dan Jacobson." I'm halfway to the gym when I hear it—my name echoing loudly over the shoddy North Hollywood High PA system. "Dan Jacobson to reception." I do a loop and head back to the office where Glennie, the old lady with the crazy curls who works the front desk, greets me.

"For you, honey." She hands me a slightly swollen manila envelope, just large enough to house a short stack of hate mail.

"Who dropped this off?" I ask, glancing out the window, hoping to catch a fast flash of Nat running away—her hair flying sideways, her plaid kilt blowing upward and back.

"Who do you mean, honey? The courier?"

I deflate. "No, sorry, I thought . . ." These past few hours of reading and reflecting has me stuck in some strange relationship vortex: *Do I hate her? Love her? Is she a vindictive psychopath? Or is she that wounded girl I once loved? The one with passion and drive and undeniable dramatic flair?* "Thanks, Glennie," I say, stepping back outside. I immediately rip into the package.

More letters, of course.

Same ribbon, same pristine cardstock.

Hey again,

So here's the part in our story where you stop loving me and start resenting me.

Flashback three months. We were in my room on your laptop, scrolling backwards through footage you'd shot the previous night. You and Ryan's mother had taken Ryan to visit a postsecondary vocational program, and Ryan had thrown a fit. He'd cried and screamed and hid behind his hands and now you were wondering whether you should use the footage you'd shot. It wasn't "upbeat enough," you were saying, staring at the computer screen while rubbing your face in frustration. "This should be a triumph for him, you know? It's a really well-run program, they get these kids paid jobs at local businesses, it's clean, it smells good, the woman who runs the place is insanely passionate and committed and——"

"Right, but . . ." I watched you sideways. Weren't there limits to documentary filmmaking? Unexpected plot twists and obstacles? "Isn't your job as a documentarian to, like, go where the story takes you?"

Your head snapped around to look at me. "Yes, of course. But there has to be some growth. A character arc. Ryan can't just go from happy to completely miserable."

"Why not?" I said, a little indignantly. "I mean if that's reflective of real life?"

"Because you don't get into USC film school by bumming the shit out of the admissions board."

I touched the mouse pad lightly, sliding backwards a few frames to a still shot of Ryan's mother holding back tears. "How could you not include this?" I asked, leaning closer to the screen. She looked so tired and sad, her mascara bleeding into the creases by her eyes, her lips riding that slim line between sad smile and frown. "This is real life and it's completely compelling. She's terrified because her kid's been at the same school since he was six and now he's a grown man with zero support system who can't take care of himself. Why can't this be your story, Dan?" I pointed at Jane Espinosa's frozen face. "THIS."

"No."

I laughed. I didn't mean to, but your response caught me off guard. "Why not?"

"Because that's not the story I want to tell. This movie is about Ryan, Natalie, not Jane Espinosa. It's about resilience in the face of adversity, and I feel like you're trying to make me make a whole other movie."

"I'm not trying to do anything," I said, touching your leg lightly. "It was just a suggestion."

You shrugged me off. "You don't ever just 'suggest' anything."

"What's that supposed to mean?"

"This is the same shit we're ALWAYS fighting about. You think you know better."

"No," I said, laughing at the absurdity. "YOU think I know better. I'm just throwing shit out into the ether and seeing what sticks."

You slammed your computer shut. "I'm going home."

"What? WHY?" I jumped up. "I thought we were gonna get dinner after this."

"Lost my appetite."

"Seriously?" I said as you stood. "You can't leave." I ran around you and blocked the door.

"Natalie, move."

"No."

"You're being a baby."

"I'M the baby?" I said, irate. "You're the guy with the massive ego who can't handle a DROP of constructive criticism."

Well that did it. You went red, veins popping, jaw rock-hard. "Natalie—" You tucked your laptop under one arm and darted left. "MOVE." I blocked you again so you went right. If you hadn't been so pissed and I hadn't been so desperate, this would've been funny. The two of us flitting back and forth in an awkward, stilted dance.

"You're ALWAYS leaving," I said, frantic for you to stay. "If something's too deep or too real or if there's even the slightest threat of conflict, you're out."

"Yeah, because you're crazy and it's terrifying."

I looked at you, stunned. This was my cue to back down like I always did when we fought. To surrender. To cry and flail and beg your forgiveness. That's how I'd always kept things right with us when things went out of whack. And you seemed to like me a little more when I was playing the flailing damsel.

But I was sick of it.

So this time when you reached for the door I grabbed your face and kissed you. It was an impulse move and I expected you to pull away but you *didn't, you BIT back.*

"Ow!" I said, wincing, my hand flying to my face. "What the hell?"

The air between us felt charged and hot, and you watched me, silent, for a long beat.

And then.

Well.

There's no nice way to say what happened next, Dan.

We hate-fucked.

We kept our clothes on and it was rough and impersonal and you—my good-guy boyfriend, the guy who had never slept with anyone BUT me—made me feel like a complete and total whore.

N

This is how we started sweeping shit under the rug. With sex.

At first it seemed like we'd discovered the great panacea; the cure-all for everything from petty grievances to true, deep despair. If Nat was being a raging bitch, it was fine, we'd fuck it out! A fight over Arielle Schulman or some sort of setback with my movie? No problem, a quick bonk and alakazam! Issue solved. Every wrong could be righted with some low-impact acrobatics; every pain dulled with a hate-fueled fuck. It worked like the ultimate magic bullet until one day it didn't. Until the thrill of makeup sex—*of near-breakup sex*—was suddenly gone.

"Dan, you want cake?"

"Sure," I said to Nat, who was next to me now sucking frosting off her thumb. I took the plate and glanced quickly across the table at the tiny Fierro clan: just Mae and Mariella. Per usual, Nat's dad was away on business. China this time, I think. Or maybe it was Taiwan.

"Can I finally pop the cork on that bottle of Veuve Clicquot?" Nat said to Mae, her eyes big with giddy delight.

"No freaking way!" Mae said, absentmindedly wiping cake crumbs off her shirt with a damp paisley bandana.

"Can I please have *something* alcoholic?"

"Natalie."

"This is a big deal!"

It *was* a big deal. The Fierros had just learned that Natalie had been handpicked to participate in the Young Arts Program at MOCA—a year-long, highly selective, *paid* position where teens get to work with museum professionals on current exhibitions. This was the big next step that Nat had been waiting for. She'd get to immerse herself in the art world and learn the inner workings of the contemporary museum system. She'd get to make things and plan parties and hang with famous people, and it would only be a matter of time before she'd dump me and take up with some bullshit conceptual artist who would somehow catapult her and her fledgling career to next-level superstardom status. I was outrageously jealous and thoroughly disgusted with myself. To compensate, I was smiling like an insane person.

"What's wrong with your face?" Nat asked, her mouth stuffed with berries and whipped cream.

"My face?"

"Yeah," she said, swallowing, sucking the tip of her plastic spork. "You look, like, crazy."

"I'm just happy for you."

"That's what happy looks like?"

My stomach dropped and my fork followed. "I'll be back," I said.

"Wait, where're you going?" She was clutching the neck of a bottle of Pellegrino. It was a poor substitute for Veuve Clicquot and she looked disappointed.

"I need to make a quick phone call," I told her, which was a lie of course. I just needed an excuse to get away and be alone for a while.

Fifteen minutes later Nat was hanging in her bedroom doorway, arms folded, watching me. "Did I ever tell you about Mariella's divorce?"

I sat up. I'd been lying on Nat's bed on my back, absentmindedly scrolling through Arielle Schulman's Instagram feed. "Mariella was married?"

"For five years, yeah. Second marriage." She shut the door and came in and sat by me on the edge of the bed. "They broke up two years ago after Mari found the guy having *relaciones sexuales* with her eighteen-year-old daughter."

"Whoa."

"Right? She'd been living in Mexico City with her dad and had just moved in with them a month earlier." Nat looked at me. "So anyways, Mari stabbed him."

"*What?*" I was certain I'd heard wrong. Nat's face was so placid and serene. "She *stabbed* him?"

"Yeah. Like with one of those small serrated steak knives."

"Holy shit."

"He didn't die or anything. And he didn't press charges because he'd screwed her kid." Nat watched her lap and played with a small rip in her jeans. "But anyways, that's *that* story."

I paused for a beat, suspicious. "Why are you telling me this?"

"Because. I know this may sound crazy, but I can kind of understand how things get that bad. How they can escalate so easily. Like, how *our* fights can get." She gave me a significant look.

I laughed, taken aback. "You got something serrated in your pocket . . . ?"

"No," she said, stony-faced. "But I've gotten physical with you before."

"Oh," I said, smiling through my discomfort. "So we're gonna talk honestly about this now?"

She sat back and shrugged. "You're pissed about the MOCA thing."

"Yeah," I said. She knew how I felt; why hide it?

"So how do we fix that?"

There was nothing to fix. Nat was winning at life, and I felt emasculated and threatened. "We don't."

"Because I'm not gonna turn down the internship for you."

"Did I say you should?"

"You don't have to say it. I know it's what you want."

Was it? I mean, the damage had already been done. Whether she took the job or not she'd already gotten the boost of validation that came with beating out thousands of other applicants. "I'm happy for you," I told her.

She let out a short, fake laugh. "No you're not."

True. This was tension you could stab with a steak knife.

And yet.

No one was screaming.

Nat wasn't throwing punches.

We weren't madly screwing in some vain effort to fix our broken relationship.

Because this was the problem that fucking couldn't fix.

"I'm going back downstairs, okay?" She was standing now, her jaw locked, her smile frozen in an insincere C-shape. "Mae wants to watch a five-hour Swedish miniseries from the seventies called *Scenes from a Marriage*."

"That's Bergman," I said, not moving, grabbing my phone off the nightstand. "It's actually really famous."

"That's what I hear. So are you coming?" she asked, shoving the door open with her bare foot. She was backlit now, a few frizzy hairs catching hallway light. She looked haloed. Sainted. I punched in my password and pulled up Arielle Schulman's Instagram feed again.

"I'll be down in a minute," I said, double-tapping a photo of Ari in a blue bikini.

To: Nathan Harmon

From: Dan Jacobson

Hi Nate,

My name is Dan Jacobson and I'm an aspiring filmmaker. Mae Fierro gave me your email and suggested I get in touch. I've seen all your movies and absolutely loved your latest, "Preach." I too have an interest in religious extremes, and I deeply enjoyed the film's exploration of Christian fundamentalism.

I don't know if Mae has mentioned me before, but I'm a senior at North Hollywood High and am currently working on a short documentary about young man with severe developmental delays. I'm also in the process of applying to your alma mater, the School of Cinematic Arts at USC. I'd love to meet you for a coffee to discuss filmmaking if you'd be willing.

Looking forward to your reply.

Best,

Dan Jacobson

To: Nathan Harmon

From: Dan Jacobson

Hi again, Nate.

A few weeks ago I sent you an email re: the possibility of meeting for coffee to discuss filmmaking/your experience at USC. I wanted to follow up. Hope all's well with you. Really looking forward to hearing back.

My best,
Dan Jacobson

OCTOBER 27, 2016, THURSDAY, 12:54 P.M., TEXT

Dan: Heads up, Schulman. That shirt you're wearing is completely see-through.

Arielle: That's the point, pervert. Enjoy it.

13

You ready for this one, Dan?

I'm in your garden right now surrounded by succulents, watching Jessa and her internet friend screw around on the porch with a selfie stick. Remember how this story starts? It was a few nights after the MOCA standoff, and I was so desperate to see you that I scaled the garden trellis and crawled through your window at two a.m. Shameful, I know, since I'd stayed so strong while you'd sulked like a child over my internship coup, but now that some time had passed I was missing you again. Pathetic? Romantic?

"Dan?"

You woke up groggy and annoyed and like, "Seriously, Nat?" But then I kissed you and put my hands in certain places, and you got all happy and horny and semi-malleable and seemed willing to let me spend the night.

"I have to be up in four hours," you said after a few minutes of lackluster *kissing.*

"So? Don't take the train then, I'll drive you and that'll give us extra time."

"But you'll miss first period."

"I'd rather be with you."

"Let's just sleep, okay?"

That stung, Dan. When had you ever chosen sleep over sex? "Oh come on," I said, hiding my hurt; grabbing the waistband of your shorts and pulling you close. You laughed uneasily and disentangled yourself before burying your head under a pillow.

My heart sank. "Why don't you wanna be with me?"

"I do," you insisted, reemerging with an evasive grin. "I just want to be with you while we sleep."

Well that wasn't good enough, Dan. I felt wounded and unwanted, and if you weren't going to prop me up then I was going to take you down. "What kind of guy turns down sex?"

Your body went rigid. "I dunno," you snapped back, your expression suddenly icy. "What kind of girl climbs through windows at night, begging to be fucked?"

My jaw smacked the floor.

"You don't want to be with a girl who likes sex, Dan." I grabbed my phone and got out of bed. "You want to date a vestal virgin."

Well that embarrassed you. You went red-faced and started backpedaling.

"That's not what I meant. You provoked me."

This is why I never told you about my past.

It's why I lied about being chaste and pure.

I'd always feared moments like this one, when you'd see me for who I truly was: a deviant. A dirty girl. "If I ask you something right now will you be completely honest with me?"

You nodded, steeling yourself.

"Swear to me."

"I swear," you said, and I wondered why I'd even come here in the first place. Had it been so unreasonable to expect that you'd be happy to see me? That we could make things right after the thing with MOCA? "Are you repulsed by me?"

"No," you insisted, and you sounded sincere but I didn't believe you.

"Do you wanna break up?"

"Natalie."

"Answer me."

"No."

"But you won't even touch me."

"It's just late, Nat."

"You think I'm slutty?"

"Natalie, stop it." You grabbed me and pulled me back to bed.

I was so worn out, Dan. So sick of trying, of fighting, so sick of being sick.

"Okay," I said, lying down, just wanting you to hold me again; wanting everything to go back to how it was in the beginning when I was new and you were new and our relationship was full of hope.

In the morning things seemed better.

"Take this," you said as I was heading out. It was your favorite fleece-lined jacket. "It's cold, okay?" You kissed me with minty lips and slipped it over my bare shoulders. I nodded and kissed back and apologized for the night before. "I shouldn't have surprised you like that," I said, and you said something like, "That's okay," but you didn't say sorry yourself. The jacket was shiny and rain resistant but soft and warm on the inside. It smelled faintly of that cologne you never wear—the woody/soapy one? I sniffed the lining, stuck my hands in the pockets, and felt something sleek and square. "Hey, your phone." I pulled it out and a picture of us from the previous spring lit the home-screen. My knees went weak. We'd been so happy then—the two of us by the beach, squinting against the sun; wavy, windswept strands of hair blowing sideways across our faces. "Can I send this to myself?"

You grabbed your cell and your eyes crinkled warmly. "That was a good day," you said, punching in your password and passing the phone back. Immediately, a text exchange popped up.

"Dan?"

You had your back turned. You were jamming your camera and all your school-supply crap into your book bag. "Hmm?"

My vision blurred. My head got hot. I quickly scanned the conversation thread: "Please wear something obscene to school tomorrow"?! It was the elf again. Just twelve hours earlier you'd been sending lewd texts to that skanky fucking elf.

Well, I just about lost my goddamn mind.

"You're a liar and a coward!" I screamed, throwing your phone clear *across the room.*

You whipped around, confused. "Hey! What's your problem?!"

"I asked you over and over again if you wanted to break up, and you swore you wanted to be with me. You SWORE it. You told me on that hike that us taking time apart was just about perspective and boundaries, but I knew you were lying. I knew it!" I ran for the door but you full-body-blocked me.

"Natalie, stop it." You were gripping my wrists now, which really flipping HURT. "What the hell is happening right now?"

"How's Arielle, Dan?"

Well, that shut you up. Your face went paper white. "We haven't done anything yet."

"YET? Oh my GOD." I yanked my hands back and rolled my eyes. "Move."

"I'm sorry!"

"You're SORRY?!"

"Can you please just"—you waved a finger in front of my face—"not scream? Jessa's asleep still and—"

"I don't give a shit if your sister can hear us!" I reached for the door again. You swung left, throwing an arm out. "Get out of the way."

"Just let me explain."

"That you screwed someone else, which is why you won't screw me?" I whacked your arm sideways. "Spare me, please." I yanked hard on the doorknob and made a run for it.

"I didn't screw anyone!"

"I don't believe you."

"Natalie!"

"WHAT?!" I stopped at the foot of the staircase and stared at you. I felt horrible and high—completely jacked on adrenaline and feelings of vindication.

"Don't leave like this."

"You don't love me, Dan."

And Dan? You fucking HESITATED. *"I do."*

"Okay, you know what?" I jiggled the lever on the screen door, my heart racing. *"Your movie is a twee pile of shit. Go fuck yourself."* I rushed outside to the Buick and ran right into a pocket of cool, biting air. Then I got in my car, turned the ignition, and slammed the gas pedal.

"Natalie!" you shouted as I screeched and bopped down your potholed driveway.

I heard you, Dan, I did, but I didn't stop driving. I cut a sharp left then a quick right and—poof!—you disappeared from view.

Nat

Gross, right? But accurate. Everyone's nightmares confirmed in under sixty seconds of high-octane drama. My movie was a quaint pile of shit and Nat finally had confirmation that something was happening with Arielle. Only *nothing* was happening with Arielle. Nothing physical anyway. It'd only ever been a bit of innocent flirting—a text here, a wink there. Ari was like a shot of sugar when I was feeling depleted; a quick pick-me-up when I felt dim in the shadow of Nat's oppressive light. But Nat didn't want to hear any of that. She'd resorted to her usual MO of name-calling and hysteria, and then before I knew it we were unexpectedly *over*. We *were* over, weren't we? I mean, no one had explicitly said the words, but how do you bounce back from that kind of nastiness?

And what was I supposed to do after she'd driven off, anyway? Wait? Go after her? Give her space? Go to school? I felt paralyzed and numb, like some sort of anesthetized, lobotomized zombie-bot. I stood on the grass for a while just waiting for something to change. Then I went back inside and grabbed my backpack and headed down the hill to the bus stop. I didn't know what else to do.

By the time I got to school I'd missed the first half of trig, so I spent the rest of first period on a bench behind the auditorium. Each message I sent to Nat went unanswered. What if she'd done something stupid? What if she was drunk on the 405 at eight a.m.? My heart sputtered and skipped like a backfiring car. I felt crazy. Restless. I texted Ruby:

D: Where are you right now?

R: World lit. Why?

D: I think Nat and I may have just broken up.

R: Holy shit.

R: Like for real?

R: I'm open next period. Walk me to 7-Eleven and I'll cheer you up. Buy you a Slurpee?

R: Dan, you okay?

D: I've got a chem quiz next period and I've already skipped calc.

R: Well, whatever you want.

What I wanted was to shut my brain off; to quit this nonsense with Natalie where every fight circled back to my inadequacy and her volatility. I wanted to stop resenting her successes. I wanted to be the better person but I also wanted the freedom to be a screwup. I was, I *am*, only seventeen after all. Don't I get a pass for being reckless and immature?

D: Toss in a fifth of whiskey and some french fries and you've got yourself a deal.

R: We'll be blitzed by lunch. You sure you wanna throw the whole day away?

I thought about it. But then I realized that the key to all this freedom business was to just say screw it and not think.

∼

We didn't go to 7-Eleven. We went to a liquor store on Colfax where Ruby paid a homeless guy ten bucks to buy us a bottle of bourbon. Then we walked two more blocks to the Jewish deli where we got sandwiches and Cokes and took those to the park for a midmorning boozy picnic.

"So, are we gonna talk about it?" Ruby asked after her first sloppy bite of roast beef. Her parents lived on sea vegetables and Buddhist ideals, so she really relished any chance she got to eat processed meat.

"I mean, sure?" I said, my stomach tensing and rolling. I'd hoped I'd be a little drunker than this by the time Ruby got around to asking questions, but—"Nat found some messages on my phone from Arielle Schulman."

Ruby's face fell. "Oh, Dan."

"We haven't done anything! It's just been a bunch of, like, dumb, shitty texts."

"Sexts?"

"Not even! Well, not really."

She shook her head.

"Don't do that. Don't give me that look."

"You just"—she sucked some dressing off her thumb—"you can't do that kind of thing. You can't commit to one girl and mess around with someone else. You two should've broken up a long time ago."

I shrugged. Ruby pulled out the bottle of bourbon and

spiked both our Cokes. "Do you feel relieved at all?" she asked, chewing her straw and watching me sideways.

I thought about the night before. About the sex we'd almost had. About the bad feelings I'd felt and the hateful thing I'd said about her begging for it. "I mean, honestly? I feel guilty."

"Don't. She's an emotional vampire." She took another sip of soda then said, "You're a good guy."

What kind of girl begs to be fucked?

What kind of girl begs to be fucked?

What kind of girl begs to be fucked?

"No," I said, pouring an extra shot or three into my icy Coke. "I'm really not."

Later, drunker, we ended up back at Ruby's for some vegan ice cream and shitty TV.

"You want whipped cream?" she asked, swaying a little, aiming the spray can at my face before redirecting it at the bowl.

"That can't be the real stuff."

"It's made with rainbows and bean curd." Giddy, she sprayed a soft cloud of soy onto my plate. "Cherry?"

I shook my head and felt some happy sloshing between my ears. A fourth a bottle of booze gone, and I was pleasantly numb. "Can we watch something scary?"

"What, like, home movies?" She licked some cream off her hand. "Get the napkins, will you?"

Ruby's house always smelled like rice. Her mother was a macrobiotic zealot, and there was a cooker in the kitchen that ran around the clock. The shelves in the living room were cluttered with crystals, totems, and paperback books about enlightenment. There were plants everywhere too—hanging, creeping, propped up in corners; the biggest ones got space on the deck. "What time's your mom back?" I asked, settling in on the couch; devouring a bite of mint chocolate chip.

"Not until six." She grabbed the remote and slid her feet under my butt. "We're going scary, huh?" She switched on the TV and scrolled through the digital queue. "Torture horror? Paranormal? Monster movie?"

"Do you wear makeup?" I asked. It was a drunk question. A dumb one.

"I'm sorry, what?" Her eyes were dancing with amusement and suspicion. "Why do you even care?"

"I don't know," I said, laughing along. "But specifically, like, on your lips?" They were so plump and soft-looking; the color of a day-old bruise. "Do you do anything special to make them that way?"

"*What* way?" she asked, blushing, mindlessly touching her mouth. "You mean like lip gloss?"

Natalie wore a gloss that I liked a lot. It smelled like cake batter and made our mouths stick together when we kissed. "Yours look purple."

"My lips?"

"Yeah," I said, thinking about different sorts of kisses: sweet ones, French ones, the ones you give babies and stuffed animals. I wondered idly what it would feel like to kiss Ruby. "Did anything ever happen with you and that old dude you dated?" Old Dude had been a junior at UCLA.

"You mean did I give it up to my college boyfriend?" She waited for me to say something snide back, but when I didn't she went, "I'm waiting for the right guy."

I felt something familiar bubbling up; something animal and ugly. "Who's that?" I asked, even though I already knew the answer; I knew how Ruby felt about me. How she'd always felt.

"You gonna make me say it?"

No, worse. I was gonna make her prove it.

I pushed aside a couch cushion and kissed her. Knowing full well it was wrong. Ruby was tanked; I was only six hours out of an insane, all-consuming, frenetic, horrible, thrilling, terrifying relationship with a girl who may or may not have been the love of my life. I was heartbroken. I was horny. I was disillusioned and drunk and I wanted to do it so I did. And I *should* regret it but I can't because here's the thing—sometimes a kiss is just a kiss, and sometimes it's this:

Ruby's hands were in my hair and her lips were soft and parted and she tasted sweet and felt so warm and each time our mouths met I felt tiny shocks and tingles. Our legs got mixed up, our shirts came off, everything was suddenly really slick—tacky skin and damp hands and I was crazy aroused so I gripped her hips and she moaned a little and then we were kissing faster and touching more and she was whispering something into my mouth, she was saying, "It's okay, I want to," and I knew what she meant, knew she wanted me to be her first. Which was flattering but *horrifying* because what the hell was I doing? This was *Ruby*, my best friend, and *Natalie*—my girlfriend? ex-girlfriend?—had been in my bed that very same morning. "We can't," I said, breaking away.

"Why can't we?" She was breathing fast still, looking messy and splotchy and so, so pretty.

"Because, Rubes, we just can't." I glanced over, shamefaced. "I'm sorry."

Her eyes were brimming with shiny tears. "Sophomore year it was Ginny Schecter, and then after her it was that girl from Crossroads, and then all of a sudden there was Natalie—screwed up and stuck up and rich." She swiped at her nose roughly. "Why wasn't it ever me?"

"Because you were, you *are*, my friend."

"So?"

"So there's a lot more at stake with you."

"That's bullshit, Dan." She looked so sad and defeated. "That's just some line that people say to each other in movies."

She was right, it *was* a line. And why *hadn't* it ever been her?

Ruby made me feel secure and loved, and Nat had always left me feeling shitty and resentful.

No contest, right?

It was the Buick I saw first, parked between the garage and Dad's succulent garden.

"Hi," Nat said. She was curled up in the wicker loveseat on the front porch, clutching her knees to her chest.

"Hi," I said back, walking slowly and with trepidation. The bourbon buzz had finally worn off, and, feeling nauseated and exhausted, the reality of what I'd just done was setting in.

"I just need to know," she said, getting up, "if you fucked the elf."

She meant Ari of course, but Ruby's face was flashing in my mind on a torturous loop. "No," I said. "I told you. It was just a few dumb texts. When you and I fight, Ari and I flirt. That's it."

"You swear."

"I swear."

"You never touched that girl?"

"Not once."

"Swear on your mother."

I hesitated a second then took the line of least resistance. "I swear on my mother."

Nat's posture softened. "I didn't mean what I said about your movie."

I was suddenly, inexplicably *weeping*. Hunched over, hands covering my wet face, crying like a kid.

Nat wrapped her arms wrapped around me, rubbing my back while whispering, "It's okay . . ." Her soft, clean hair brushed against my sweaty, sticky face.

"No it's not."

"It is. Dan. Look at me."

I looked at her.

"Why are you crying?"

"I don't know," I said. Was it the fight from earlier? Or maybe the guilt I felt about my slip up with Ruby? "I'm sorry."

"I'm sorry too." She wiped my wet cheeks. "Do you want to be with that girl?"

I didn't, so, "No."

"Do you want to be with me still?"

I honestly wasn't sure. "Yes."

"You smell like booze," she said.

"Drinking lunch."

She kissed my neck and after that my cheeks and lips. All the places Ruby had kissed earlier. "Nat . . ." My stomach churned with shame.

"Put your arms around me," she commanded softly. "Please, Dan? Can we please just pretend this morning never happened?"

I slid my arms around her waist and squeezed hard. "Okay," I said, wondering if maybe I'd been granted some sort of reprieve. We'd fought, I'd been confused, I'd done something stupid. But maybe we could bounce back from this one tiny indiscretion?

"Dan, you're shaking."

"I think I'm hungover."

"Tell me you love me."

"I love you."

"Say it again."

"I love you."

"One more time."

"I love you, Nat."

From: Arielle Schulman

To: Dan Jacobson

Ari: Sometimes when Whitman disappoints me I wonder about you. If you and I could love each other if we didn't already love other people. I fantasize about you sometimes. Do you ever fantasize about me?

Dan: Constantly.

Dan: Please wear something obscene to school tomorrow.

Ari: X.

14

Dan,

Seven weeks ago, sixteen months into our relationship, you and I went to our first and only fairy-tale ball together. The flowers, the formal wear, the pink stretch limos! Those Valley kids really know how to party it up in —
what? Not style exactly—stripper stilettos, maybe? Carnation corsages?
In lieu of driving all the way over the hill to re-create the experience, I'm relaxing right now in the lobby of the haunted, historic Biltmore Hotel downtown; curled up on an overstuffed loveseat, sipping a virgin piña colada on a school night.

What follows is a dramatic reenactment. I'll be playing the role of VICTIM.

FADE IN:

INT. BURBANK MARRIOTT—BANQUET HALL—NIGHT
Senior prom in the San Fernando Valley. Strobe lights, pop music,

169

corporate hotel décor. Girls in shiny dresses prance in packs on a vinyl dance floor. Sweaty boys in tuxes swill whiskey from gleaming flasks.

BEN WHITMAN, tall and cocksure, slaps hands with DAN JACOBSON, an insecure little two-timing piece of shit. Whitman's girlfriend, ARIELLE SCHULMAN—wicked, wanton, epically slutty—gives Dan a sloppy, lingering cheek kiss.

VICTIM, A.K.A. ME, keels over and dies.

I wanted to murder you, Dan. A fucking kiss? The audacity! The flagrant flirting! I shot Schulman the lousiest look I could muster and she cowered and shrunk and I instantly knew you two were screwing. I pulled you aside and said, "You're a liar."

And you went red but stayed stoic. "Don't do this, Natalie. Don't wreck tonight."

But it was already wrecked, Dan. I'd seen the way she looked at you and the way you avoided her looks. "Just tell me," I said.

"Tell you what?"

"That you're fucking her."

"I hate when you talk like that."

So I screamed FUCK in your face and took off, my veins throbbing with heat. And you chased after me, insisting that there was nothing going on with you two. But I wanted a confession so I tried a softer tactic: "I just need you to be honest with me," I said, reaching for your clammy hand. "I can handle the cheating; I just can't handle you lying about it."

And you were like, "I'm not lying," but you were, Dan! You were! And then Ruby and this other chick appeared out of nowhere. Ruby looked sad and her friend looked MAD and neither one of them stopped to say hi or even glance our way but I knew that they'd seen us because I KNOW SHIT and then that's when it hit me: maybe you hadn't been lying about Arielle after all. Maybe I'd been worried about the wrong girl all along.

"Ruby looks really pretty tonight," I said, testing you. She and her friend had just disappeared into the bathroom.

"Does she?" You glanced around, shrugging coolly. "I haven't seen her yet."

Really, Dan? Hadn't you noticed the pink glossy lips and the flat-ironed hair? Her sexy little poly-blend prom dress? After all, this was the girl you'd known since you were thirteen. The one who'd vacationed once with your family in Mammoth. The one you left me for in Joshua Tree. How had you missed her super conspicuous drive-by?

"I'm leaving," I said, alarm bells blaring in my brain.

"Are you kidding me? Natalie, it's PROM."

"So what?" I said, ripping off my corsage.

"Hey!" You caught my arm and pulled me close. "Don't do this."

"Be honest with me."

"I AM being honest with you."

"Bullshit," I said, shaking loose and walking away.

The girl Nat's talking about, the one with Ruby that night in the Marriott lobby? That was Sue Jablonski, Ruby's scariest friend.

Sue's always been pretty stuck up and stern, but right around the time that Ruby and I hooked up Sue started ignoring me outright. Shooting me death looks at school; hugging Ruby close whenever I passed by. Mutual friends wanted to know what I'd done to piss Jablonski off—had I stolen her lunch money? Her pencil case? And why hadn't Ruby and I been hanging out lately? What had happened to our devout commitment to each other? To our rock-solid friendship?

Sex happened, of course. Or something close to it.

It had wormed its way into the grooves of our relationship and tainted everything. I can only guess at what Ruby must have said to Sue about our encounter. That I'd been careless, maybe. Or worse, that I'd been heartless. And she wouldn't be wrong, would she?

"Just cut the girl loose, Dan."

Jessa was at the kitchen counter hunched over a bowl of leftover carbonara, offering up unsolicited advice about my relationship. "Seriously, I don't understand why you and Natalie just don't break up."

"I think we love each other."

"You think?"

I wasn't sure. Was this what love was? A relationship rife with resentment and infidelity? I winced with guilt, flashing back to my afternoon with Ruby. "I sort of did something."

"You and Lefèvre got it on."

"No!"

"No?"

"Sort of?"

"Dan!"

"I mean, we didn't *sleep* together, but—wait, how do you know that?"

"Because I have *eyes*, loser! Because you've been stringing that girl along for-fucking-*ever*."

I swallowed a golf ball. "Is that true?"

"Dan."

The reality of what I'd done was suddenly hitting me like an avalanche. "Nat knows. I swear she knows. I mean, maybe not the specifics exactly? But she's been asking me a ton about this one girl, and I just think, like, *psychically* she somehow senses that I've messed around and—"

"Oh God, stop," Jessa said, her arms crisscrossed over her head protectively. "Just stop whining and be a grown-up. Do you want to be with her?"

"Who?"

She whacked my head hard. "Your girlfriend, dumbass!"

"I don't know."

"Well, what about Ruby?"

I shrugged helplessly. I wasn't sure about her either. "I have to tell Nat. I feel so bad."

"Yeah, *you* feel bad but that's your problem. Do you really wanna go and make Natalie feel worse?" She shoveled a spoonful of peas into her mouth.

"I thought you said we should break up."

"You should. But telling her that you screwed your best friend isn't going to make things any better."

"We didn't screw."

Jessa looked at me like I'd just smashed the contents of her makeup drawer. "Do you hear yourself?"

"Barely?"

"It doesn't matter if you actually had sex," she said, pushing the last of her cold carbonara aside. "Why'd you do it anyways? Like, do you actually have feelings for Ruby?"

"No," I said, quickly, *reflexively*, and then, "I mean, I don't know." I tried looking inward to see if my heart or gut or *spleen* had any insight. "I think I did it to feel better about myself."

"Oh God." Her lips settled into a sober, straight line. "You're horrible."

I flinched, stung. "No, I'm not."

She watched me now, her eyes tiny; her head wagging slowly in stark disbelief. "No, you are, really. Go look up D-bag in the dictionary, Dan. Your picture's right there, wedged between two shirtless photos of Bieber."

"Jess."

"You're the reason I don't date."

"Don't say that."

"It's true."

I laughed uneasily, hoping a little levity might offset my discomfort and Jessa's rage. No luck. Her icy eyes radiated a steady beam of contempt.

"You look just like Mom when you're mad," I said with a smile, thinking some flattery might smooth things over. And it did. Jessa softened instantly, her shoulders dropping and her eyebrows bouncing up.

"I hate you."

She was grinning now so I seized my opportunity—pulling her quickly into a tight embrace. "No, you don't."

"I do."

"Jess."

"Please be a better guy, Dan."

"I'm trying."

"Try harder," she said, sighing loudly, disentangling herself from our hug. She grabbed her camera off a nearby step stool held it out to me. "Here, take it. I need you to shoot my 'What I Ate in a Day' video."

"Didn't you just eat?"

"You think I'm gonna post a video of me slurping a massive bowl of cold carbonara on the internet? No, Dan, come on, time to make an acai bowl."

"A what?"

"Can you just film me while I blend shit?"

I winced, guilty. "I can't? I still need signatures from three sets of Dayview parents so I can shoot Ryan's commencement."

"It'll take three seconds."

"Jess . . ."

"Three seconds." She shook the camera in my face. "Just take it, okay? If you help me, I'll help you."

"You will?"

"Yeah, they're not calling you back, right? So we'll go out together and try some door-to-door salesmanship. You'll seem much less threatening with a sixteen-year-old angel on your arm." She reached into the freezer and pulled out an armful of unidentifiable frozen fruits. "So what's your elevator pitch?"

I froze, suddenly seized with performance pressure. "Okay, so, here are these kids, right? Working hard to set up a sustainable life post-graduation. Their parents want them to be as independent as possible, but it's so much bigger than that. It's about legislation and funding for community programs. It's about getting retail stores to partner with autism advocacy groups, and—"

Jessa yawned.

"I'm boring you?"

"Oh, to tears."

"You got a better suggestion?"

"Yep." She tossed a bag of shredded coconut onto the kitchen counter and smiled. "So, like, why are you making this movie? In a sentence. Without using phrases like 'autism advocacy' or 'legislation.'"

"What do you mean, *why*?"

"I mean exactly that: *why*?"

"Because Ryan's story is important. Because he's facing issues that all kids with autism face."

"But why Ryan specifically?"

I hated when she got like this. Patronizing and challenging. "You know I'm the older one, right?"

"You're sure?"

"I don't know why I picked him. Because his family was amenable to the idea?"

"Wrong."

"Because he's my favorite kid at Dayview?"

"Exactly!" Jessa slapped my back enthusiastically. "Now let's go knock on doors and tell people that a single story is all you need to make big waves of change! Tell them that you want these kids to live in a world that sees them as whole individuals, not just as issues or mascots. You're trying to move people, right? Like, you want people to empathize with Ryan and his family?"

"Yeah, of course."

"So that's all you need to say." She waved a hand at her camera. "Shoot me."

I stared back, speechless. "You're so much smarter than me it makes me sick."

"Hello! Start filming so I can start blending! I've already got five thousand subscribers, Dan! I'm building my brand!"

My cell chimed. I reached for it and read the text preview.

We need to talk.

It was from Natalie.

MARCH 26, 2017, SUNDAY, 10:02 A.M., TEXT

From: Matt Libby

To: Dan Jacobson

Your sister could sell salt to a slug. I'll send the signed form with Fiona to school tomorrow.

MARCH 26, 2017, SUNDAY, 2:53 P.M., EMAIL

From: Liza Wheeler

To: Dan Jacobson

Hi, Dan.

Jen and I talked it over, and we're on board. See attached. Consent signed and dated.

Best,

Liza Wheeler

MARCH 27, 2017, MONDAY, 6:55 A.M., EMAIL

From: Laura Villet, cc: Brian Villet

To: Dan Jacobson

Here you go, Dan. Your lucky day.

Laura and Brian

15

MAY 17, 2017, WEDNESDAY, 2:12 P.M.

So, Dan, you're a smart guy, right?

I'm sure you've gleaned the subtle subtext from these letters: that I know all about your torrid affair with Ruby Ladylove Lefèvre!

You curious to hear how I found out? How I finally—after much speculation and paranoia—confirmed a growing, itching suspicion?

I hacked your email of course. Right after prom.

"Hey, Novio?"

"Hey, Nat?"

Remember that afternoon in January, pre-hike-from-hell, when we watched The Exorcist in bed on your laptop?

"Got any delicious snacks?" I asked. A possessed Linda Blair had just puked pea soup all over a priest, and I was suddenly, inexplicably starving.

"I'm sure I can scrounge something up," you said, kissing me then bouncing off the bed. "Want anything else? A crucifix, maybe? The blood

of a sacrificial lamb?"

"Please!" I paused the movie. "But with a side of whipped cream?"

You laughed and left. I wasn't sure what to do with myself so I watched the wall for a bit. I sat up and braided my hair. I thought deeply and briefly about demon possession, but after a minute or so I got antsy. "You coming back anytime soon?" I called out.

"I'm assembling a junk food platter!"

I can't really explain why I did what I did next, but when I get antsy, Dan, I just do things. I INNOCENTLY clicked on a desktop file titled "Web Crap," and just HAPPENED to glance quickly at a list of passwords, namely the one that accessed your email account.

"I come bearing processed food," you said moments later, back with a tray full of delicious and horrible treats: cheese crackers, spray cheese, tiny pickles, and frozen mini Mars Bars.

"You spoil me," I said, discreetly closing the file, grabbing a chowlate off the tray then tearing into it with my two front teeth.

Flash forward three months to three hours after prom.

I was home, hating you, feeling suspicious of you and Ruby, and I'd been sitting on your password for nearly two months. Impressive, yes? My willpower?).

No longer able to resist the alluring call of the World Wide Web of Secrets and Lies, I hurriedly typed your info into the Gmail homepage and within seconds was staring at your fully loaded inbox.

A quick search, a minute or two of scrolling and clicking, and there it was finally. Proof.

I'm not going to type up a transcription here of the Ruby exchange because I draw the line at writing letters inside of letters, but let's just say that you two had tons of FEELINGS after screwing around and Ruby just could not understand why you'd gone back to your crazy whore of a girlfriend, i.e., me.

WELL FUCK YOU BOTH VERY MUCH.

You could've cheated with anyone, Dan. A cheerleader, a prostitute, a ceramics-loving elf. Why Ruby? Why the one girl with the power to invalidate our ENTIRE RELATIONSHIP? Was she really that much better than me?

—N

Is that it, the big and final reveal? I cheated, Nat knows, and she found me out by hacking my email?

To be honest, I can't even blame her for the privacy breach. I *did* do things with Ruby and if I were her and suspected as much, I might've hacked my account too. But that can't be it, can it? There must be more. I need a conclusion, an epilogue, a denouement. It's three p.m. and school's nearly out. Do I check with reception again for more letters? Do I swing past my locker on my way to Dayview for commencement?

I haven't seen Nat since our official breakup a little over a month ago. It was sunny and cool that day at the park, like fall on some northern planet. Nat looked unexpectedly sheepish and sweet—barefaced and quiet, wearing paint-splattered ripped jeans.

"Hey," I said, greeting her quickly with an awkward kiss. It'd been two weeks since we'd last talked at prom and I still wasn't sure where we stood. Were we together? Broken up? I'd expected her to reach out like always—to call me crying or to climb through my window—she hadn't. "You okay, stranger?"

"I'm okay," she said, smiling, her eyes bouncing around distractedly. "Should we sit?"

I sat. Another minute ticked by. Nat picked up a rock, played with it, and put it back down. "I think we need to break up."

It was a wallop to the gut. I'd been expecting it, of course.

I'd even fantasized about it a bit, but I never really thought it would happen *this* way, with Nat initiating.

"What're you thinking?" she asked, squinting now, one hand blocking a skinny ray of sunshine.

Was it a trick question? "I think you're right," I said, watching her sideways with suspicion.

"Great."

"Really?" I scanned her face for signs of sadness or regret. "You really think it's great that we're breaking up?"

"I mean, we haven't spoken in weeks."

She wasn't wrong, but the lack of tears and turmoil threw me. "Nat, I'm sorry about—" What? What was I sorry for? For being a disloyal shit? I wanted to tell her that after a year and a half together we could fix this but— "I just wish things had worked out differently with us." This was true, but it still didn't seem like enough. I'd always thought we'd go down with a little more fanfare and flair.

She nodded. "Bygones, yeah?"

"Bygones?" Where was that raw, real, emotional girl I'd fallen hard for? The wild one who had me spellbound at "Pearl Jam's my jam, Dan!" The brazen one with zero filter who lived and died by the heart. *She* was the one I needed to say good-bye to. "I'll miss you," I said, meaning it, but she didn't say it back.

So I hugged her.

It was the only thing I could think to do.

And she hugged back, but limply. "I have to leave. I told Lex I'd meet her at The Grove at five."

"Okay," I said, feeling confused and desperate and reluctant to let go. "You're sure?"

"I'm sure."

"But I'll see you around?"

"You'll see me," she said, starting off.

I felt a blast of regret then blurted, "Wait!" but she didn't wait. She just kept on walking, never once turning around to look back.

To: Michael Fierro

From: Mae Fierro

Hey,

Something is seriously wrong with our kid. I'm 95% certain that she and Dan broke up, because she's barely left her room since Wednesday and she's refusing food, even rolls from Katsu-Ya. Alexa keeps stopping by with flowers and bags of all that cheap crap that they love from the 99 Cent Store. Do I try to get her in to see Ginsberg this week? Or maybe a therapist? Doesn't your mother have someone she likes on the Westside?

I thought about asking Keri for the name of her shamanic practitioner, but I figured you'd be pissed if I took our child to a witch doctor while you were away in Tokyo.

Can you pick up some of those special bean cakes for Fluff before your flight tomorrow? You know how she is about Japanese snacks.

X, M

16

DAN, 4:15 P.M.

I'm on my knees in the Dayview lobby, ransacking my camera
bag for an extra memory card, when—

"Dan?"

I glance up. It's Arthur, Dayview security, waving a skinny
manila package overhead. "Hey, man."

"Natalie dropped this off earlier."

My heart palpitates. Here it is, finally, I can feel it: Natalie's
swan song and the climax I've been craving. "She was here?"

"Yeah, about an hour ago." He hands me the envelope. "She
said to say good luck."

A chill shimmies up my spine. I stand, tuck the package
under my bag flap, and shake Arthur's hand. "Thanks, man."

"Go on back to the auditorium, okay? They're just setting
up the chairs."

It's early still, so very few families are milling about. A couple of guys from campus services are still setting up like Arthur mentioned, and there's a modest, makeshift concession stand by the exit—a table draped with nylon fabric offering bottles of water and individually wrapped protein snacks. I feel around in my bag for Nat's package then ask Jeanne Carey, principal and superhuman, if Ryan's around.

She nods enthusiastically, gesturing toward the exit with her clipboard. "He's in the senior bungalow suiting up with everyone else."

So I head back out the way I came in—down the carpeted corridor and outside to the basketball court. But instead of going to see Ryan right away, I duck quickly into the nearest boys' bathroom and—"Hello?"—check to see if I'm alone before slipping into a toilet stall to frantically fish for Nat's package. It's square and pointy and far too thin to be a sizable stack of notes. I rip into it with two hands and my breath catches a bit. Another letter of course.

But just one.

Plus a cookie. The lumpy kind I like from that bakery on Larchmont; the one Nat would always bring me on days we met at Union Station.

I lean against the cool brick of the bathroom wall and unfold her note.

So here it is, Dan—our final curtain call!

Are you ready for your closing bow? Ready for the wild and raucous applause of the crowd? I mean, you deserve it, Novio. You've turned in a Tony-award worthy performance this year—playing the good Samaritan, the loyal boyfriend, the doting son, the dependable friend. And what about me, huh? Am I by your side on that stage, curtsying like a debutante or a star thespian? Think hard, Dan, because I'd sure like to go out with a bow or a bang. I mean, who can resist a dramatic exit? Not me, clearly. I'm furiously at work right now writing our new ending—it's interactive! Care to partake?

Sometime in late February when we were still screwing like crazy, when sex was the cheap glue that was keeping us stuck together, you said: "Can I film us?"

Screwing, you meant. We'd been mid-makeout and now you wanted to film us naked and vulnerable doing obscene things to each other. My gut reacted with a fat freaking NO, but you had this goddamn GLINT in your eye, Dan. You were stroking my hair and smiling roguishly and you just seemed so excited and into me and you hadn't been either of those things in so long that instead of just saying what I wanted to say which was ABSOLUTELY NOT, I went, "What do you mean? Like right now?"

"Yeah, I've got my camera."

My stomach flipped. I'd seen this shit go wrong before: leaked celebrity sex tapes; high school nobodies with their faces/tits/splayed legs popping up on Porn Hub and RedTube. I wasn't interested in being internet smut, nor did I want my peers seeing me weak and exposed, BUT (and this is a really big BUT, Dan) I wanted to please you. I was DESPERATE to keep you. I'd never thought of myself as the pathetic, spineless, doormat type, but our relationship had turned into a messy pile of misery and while you may not have liked me anymore you sure as shit still wanted to have sex with me, so I was going to let you. Even if you wanted to film me doing it. "Maybe?" *I said.*

"Maybe?"

"Yeah, but what's, like, the point exactly?"

"I mean, don't you think it's kind of hot?"

"I guess?"

"We could watch it afterward."

"I'm not sure I want to watch myself."

"But you're so sexy," *you purred like some sort of lothario. What had happened to my squeaky clean, virgin boyfriend?*

"If we do this, you have to swear to me you'll never show it to anyone."

"But what if we want to watch it with our grandkids one day?"

I laughed and slapped you. "Promise me!"

"Okay, I promise."

"No, like, MEAN IT, Dan."

"I swear," *you said and you sounded sincere so I went,* "Okay, but you can't, like, brag about it to your friends later on. You can't be, like," *I lowered my voice,* "'Oh, I made a sex tape.'"

You were laughing now too, and it felt nice. We hadn't laughed like this in forever.

So maybe I could do this. It would be like making art, only smuttier. "All right," I said, relenting. "Sure, why not?"

And you were so excited, remember? You jumped out of bed and set up the camera and I slipped off my clothes. and what happened next was absurd and a little awkward and sometimes thrilling but embarrassing too, and when it was over I felt funny but you clearly didn't; you looked big and puffed up, exactly how Kitty Carlisle looks after she's killed some sad spider who, seconds earlier, had been creeping happily, lazily, across the living room floor.

You had the power now, Dan.

I was the prey.

It was your camera, your file, you were the man on top. I had nothing but your word, which I now know was worthless.

Because you didn't keep your promise, did you?

This is how you broke me, Dan.

And now I'm going to break you.

Meet me at the pool on the Eagle Hill side of campus at 4:30 p.m.

If you don't show I will fucking annihilate you.

Publicly.

X, Natalie

HOLY SHIT.

What a colossal fucking mistake.

How could I have missed this?

How could I have not seen the Sanskrit on the wall and put the pieces together sooner?

"Hello?"

How the hell did she find out?

And why did I insist on filming us to begin with?

What did I even *get* out of shooting that video anyway? A half an hour of cheap thrills? A few weeks' worth of whack-off material?

"Natalie?"

It was an honest slipup. One fast, false move. One careless flick of the mouse and I'd somehow managed to do the thing I *swore* I'd never do: humiliate her.

Expose her.

"Nat, you here?"

The fluorescents flicker on and Natalie steps out from behind a wall of bright metal cubbies. "Boo," she says, and I go cold. She's stunning and smiling, her eyes blazing with hot fury—two amber balls dancing in the blue light reflecting off the still pool.

"Hey," she says, and she seems super keyed up. She's shifting back and forth from leg to leg. "Did you miss me?"

192

I didn't, but I can't say that, can I? Her gaze darts to my bag, which hangs low by my hip.

"Is your camera in there?" she asks, wasting zero time. I quickly grab the strap on my bag and keep my hand there.

"Please don't," I plead. She knows nothing matters more to me than seeing this ceremony through. That Ryan's graduation is the most crucial piece of my project. That my future, that all my scholarship bullshit, that ALL OF MY SELF-WORTH— it's all tied up in this one moment. "Whatever you're about to do, you don't have to do it. You know that, right? We can talk about this."

"Just give me the bag, Dan." She sounds so easy-breezy, as if she isn't about to destroy my life, and along with it, twelve-hundred-bucks-worth of brand-new equipment.

"It was an accident," I blurt, eager to cut to the punch. "I was afraid someone would see the video on my computer so I labeled it something innocuous and stuck it in my Dayview folder. But then a few weeks ago I put together a rough cut of all the footage I had of Ryan, and I sent it to a few guys for feedback." I shrug helplessly. "Only I sent the wrong file. I'd named both 'Espinosa 2,' but one file name had an *actual* two in it and the other one had a roman numeral."

She doesn't react. She shifts again from leg to leg, her face frozen. "The camera, Dan."

I consider making a run for it, but I know that if I flee she'll just follow, surely finding a way to sabotage commencement with some sort of verbal and very public character assassination. "I felt horrible about it, Nat."

"Aw," she says, feigning pity with an exaggerated pout. "Pretty sure I felt worse."

"I only sent it to Whitman and a few other guys."

"Only?"

"And they all swore they deleted it," I say, but had they really? Nat knows about the leak after all, so maybe one of them lied? "How exactly did you . . . ?"

"Find out?"

I nod slowly. Did someone confront her? Is she still reading my emails post-breakup?

"The elf told me."

My stomach plummets. *"Arielle?"*

"Cool twist, right?"

I think back on my conversation—confrontation?—with Ari from earlier. *It's not me you should be saying sorry to.* "But *how*?" I ask. "I don't get it. How did Ari know about the tape?"

"Whitman, Dan. He thought it was fucking hilarious."

I wince. I swear to God if he were here I'd pummel him. "Nat—" I want so badly to rewind time and undo all of it— the file mishap, the video, my indiscretion with Ruby. "I'm so sorry."

"Hey, no sweat," she says with biting insincerity. "Your girl

194

Ari really came through for me. I guess she had some sort of colossal realization when she saw us screwing onscreen."

"I never meant to hurt you, or embarrass you, or—"

"*Embarrass* me?" she says, visibly pissed. "That's sort of underselling it, don't you think? I'm pretty sure what you did could be considered a criminal act in some states." Her eyes go wide and wild.

"I'm sorry."

"Stop saying that."

"But I am."

"I don't care. Do you seriously not understand how fucking terrible you are?"

I have never, ever felt guilt like this.

"Dan?"

"I don't know what else to say."

She looks at me for a long beat, and then suddenly, *finally*, she's crying. "I hate you," she whispers, her cheeks going red, her chin doing its signature quiver.

I have an overwhelming urge to hold her. "What can I do?" I ask meekly.

"Fuck off."

I get up and go to her. I know I shouldn't. I know I'm the one who's doing the hurting, but I can't stop myself. "Nat."

She falls against my chest, sobbing wildly. I touch her hair and smell her sweet scalp and rub her hot back while she cries.

"No one has ever hurt me as bad as you," she says, dotting my shirt with tears and loose lashes. "You've broken my heart, Dan."

I wrap my arms around her shoulders and squeeze hard.

And that's when it happens.

When I'm defenseless.

She slips the bag off my shoulder and tosses my camera into the water.

"Natalie, no!"

And it sinks.

And everything slows to a near stop.

Screaming, I bolt for the pool, my fists cutting the air while I run. But Nat grabs my shirt, dragging me back. "Let go," I yell, slipping on the wet tile then landing on my knees; jeans soaking up puddles of murky, chlorinated water, my legs pulsating with a sudden, searing pain.

"I had to," she says softly, bending down to meet my gaze with an apologetic look. "I had to make things right with us. Even the score, you know?"

Exhausted, *broken*, I roll sideways onto my butt, my eyes burning with the sting of defeat.

"Are you crying?" Nat asks with incredulity.

"No," I tell her. But I am. I'm completely fucking wrecked.

I inhale.

She exhales.

Our arms brush lightly while we watch the pool ripple and wave.

"I loved you so much," she says after a long beat, her voice thick with what sounds like a stuck sob.

I shake my head disbelievingly. Everything I've worked so hard for, my movie's climax, *my entire future*—she's demolished it. Or maybe I did that myself. My dreams drowned in the Eagle Hill lap pool. "We destroyed each other."

Nat blinks at me.

"No, like *really*," I say, running a hand over my face. "Like, we fucking *leveled* each other."

She smiles sadly then rests her head on my shoulder. And it feels good. Which makes me think that I'm profoundly, *deeply* screwed up.

"Dan?"

"Yeah?"

"Are you with Ruby now?"

I wince with remorse. "No, Nat. I'm not with Ruby."

We both stare into space for a bit. After a minute, Nat sits up and checks her phone. "It's nearly five," she says, twisting sideways to look at me; her face an awkward, anxious grimace. "You should go. You should tell Jane and Ryan what happened with your camera."

I disentangle myself then stand up. "I should probably fish my bag out of the pool first. My wallet's in there."

"Oh right." She bites her lip then looks around. "I'll get a net. You want help, yeah?" We lock eyes and I wonder if this is the last time I'll see her.

"Yeah," I say with a shrug, taking her hand and pulling her upright.

MAY 19, 2017, FRIDAY, 3:36 P.M., TEXT

To: Ben Whitman

From: Dan Jacobson

You're a dick, Whitman.

JUNE 21, 2017, WEDNESDAY, 6:53 P.M., EMAIL

To: Dan Jacobson

From: Jane Espinosa

Wanted to update you. Just got a call from Cheryl Levine over at Pegasus in Altadena. She got Ryan a place in their day program for the upcoming year. We're thrilled, Dan. We're celebrating at the house on Friday night if you want to stop by for some pie. Ry would love to see you.

Jane

JULY 3, 2017, MONDAY, 12:02 P.M., TEXT

To: Dan Jacobson

From Jessa Jacobson

Just ran into Ruby at the Rite Aid in Westwood. She was with that UCLA dude she used to date. THEY WERE KISSING IN THE COSMETICS AISLE!!!!!

JULY 26, 2017, WEDNESDAY, 12:20 A.M., CHAT

N_Fierro: Just got home. We mostly talked about the program and the prep work we've been doing for MOCA Teen Night. He wants to curate when he's all grown up, and he seems very enthusiastic about my work, which is nice.

AlexaMcKay17: Did you kiss?

N_Fierro: Yes, and that was nice too.

AlexaMcKay17: JUST nice?

N_Fierro: Well, I'm working on finding joy and validation within myself these days.

AlexaMcKay17: Ha. Praise Buddha.

N_Fierro: And you know, I'm never gonna be so furiously in love with this guy, so wild with desirous jealousy that I write him a sixteen-part breakup letter that culminates in sabotage, heartache, and destroyed dreams.

AlexaMckay17: Oh right.

N_Fierro: But maybe that's a good thing?

[Acknowledgments tk]